PICTURE THIS
Teaching Reading Through Visualization

PICTURE THIS
Teaching Reading Through Visualization

Laura Rose

ZEPHYR PRESS
Tucson, Arizona

PICTURE THIS
© 1989 ZEPHYR PRESS, TUCSON, ARIZONA

ISBN 0-913705-32-2

The purchase of this book entitles the individual teacher to reproduce the forms for use in the classroom. The reproduction of any part for an entire school or school system or for commercial use is strictly prohibited. No form of this work may be reproduced or transmitted or recorded without written permission from the publisher.

Book Design and Production: Kathleen Koopman

CONTENTS

Acknowledgments 6
Foreword 7
Introduction 9
      Getting Students to Read More and Enjoy It 9
      Visualization: The Missing Link in the Reading Chain ... 11
How to Use This Manual 13
      Overview 16
      Plan for the School Year 21
Evaluation 23

SECTION I: VISUALIZATION 27
    1   Preparation 29
    2   I Remember Mama 32
    3   Listen My Children and You Shall See 56
    4   Archetypes 67
    5   Characters and Settings 82
    6   Magic Journeys 86
    7   Create a Myth 102
    8   Image While You Read 117
    9   What Turtle? 122
    10   Imaging in Content Areas 127
    11   Vocabulary Books 134

SECTION II: LITERATURE 143
    12   Comprehension 145
    13   Reading and Sharing Books 151
    14   Homework Program 158
    15   Oral Reading 163

Bibliography 172

ACKNOWLEDGEMENTS

I would like to thank some of the many friends and colleagues whose ideas and encouragement have made the conception and the reality of this manuscript possible. I give special thanks to my good friend and co-worker Shirley Johnson who spent many hours with me listening, refining, and contributing. Her classroom has been a proving ground for many of the ideas set forth here, and her passionate love of children's literature has given me the faith to continue.

Thanks also go to Nancy Cox, an extraordinary Resource Specialist Teacher, whose caring and innovation have changed the lives of many of her students. The ideas that she has shared with me are reflected in many of the suggestions in this reading program.

My thanks and deep appreciation go to Jan Coates, who had the confidence in me to hire and train me to share effective teaching methods with Humboldt and Del Norte County teachers. Without Jan's support and the doors that she opened for me, this book never would have been conceived or written.

I also wish to thank some of the educational innovators whose ideas have shaped my thinking over the past ten years. Workshops by Jean Houston, George Leonard, Robert Samples, Jack Canfield, and Barbara Clark have given me ideas for visualizations and relaxations, as well as the theory and the motivation for fitting these activities into appropriate educational settings.

Lastly, I wish to thank my students, who helped me reconsider and revise this manuscript. They experienced the activities and let me know how the scripts worked in actual practice. Their enthusiasm and their successes gave me the most help of all.

FOREWORD

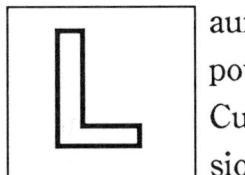aura Rose has innately and intuitively seen the profound power of imagery and visualization in the classroom. Currently marching stride for stride alongside such visionaries as Beverly Galyean, Jean Houston, Robert McKim, Rudolph Arnheim and many others, Laura began implementing her commitment to visual imagery almost as soon as she entered the field of education. She began alone and without the backing of formulated theory and research. Now theory stands firmly behind the practices she formulated from her own experience.

We now have the massive evidence of the power of guided imagery. In medicine, life-threatening illness has been effectively treated by imagery. In management, stress reduction using imagery has been instituted as a standard practice. In schooling, the quality of writing is dramatically improved at all levels. In athletics, basic skills are more readily attained. The list is endless.

Howard Gardner, a noted neuropsychologist and author of *Frames of Mind: A Theory of Multiple Intelligences*, recently said that different intelligences are ordained by design attributes in the human brain. The complex array of design features in the brain that are devoted to the visual are well known. The utilization of imagery as a standard to instruction provides a richer and more complete way for children and people of all ages to learn more authentically and creatively.

For many of us, these are ways of knowing and learning that we engaged in without any kind of validation in our growing up. Those "daydream" times and the moments when we were assumed to be "not paying attention" were times when

♣ **Foreword**

our own biological design was drawing us into realms of thought and experience that people like Laura Rose have now legitimized. Imaging is a sacred talent that we all possess. It is a gift that benefits the kindergartner, grandmother, Nobel laureate, and the artist. Laura shows us how to use this gift in ways that will help to make children lifelong learners. Picture This . . . Thank You!

Bob Samples
Boulder, Colorado

Bob Samples is an author, lecturer, seminar leader, and researcher in the fields of brain-mind function and creativity. His most recent book is *Open Mind/Whole Mind: Parenting and Teaching Tomorrow's Children Today.* It is published by Jalmar Press.

INTRODUCTION
Getting Students to Read More and Enjoy It

orking as a teacher of teachers, I have been privileged to witness the amount of caring and energy that most classroom teachers bring so generously to their work. Long hours are spent trying to teach this generation of children to read successfully. Teachers want their students to have a high level of comprehension, critical thinking ability, and enthusiasm in their reading.

Yet, despite the dedication and caring, tests seem to show that students are doing no better, and often worse, than they were twenty years ago. Or fifty years, or one hundred. Children are reading less, not more. What is going wrong?

A large part of the trouble is that the very tools that were developed to further reading achievement have instead become a powerful force in its deterioration. Worksheets, phonics drills, diagnostic tests, and continuums have become so important as indicators of reading success that in many classrooms they have nearly supplanted reading itself. Students are decoding each word, or perhaps remembering it from their store of sight words, but to them each word or phrase is merely a discrete group of sounds. They do not get the sense behind the sounds. No picture springs into their minds as the words are sequentially mouthed. Reading is not a satisfying, enjoyable activity.

✣ Getting Students to Read More

Fortunately results of new research, generating from many sources, are now becoming available to educators. Robert Ornstein, Bob Samples, and Robert Sylwester are among those who are bringing us information about the workings of the two halves of the brain. Madeline Hunter is translating decades of psychological research into principles that we can put to use in the classroom. Pioneers like Jean Houston and George Leonard are exploring how the mind, brain, and body work together for effective learning. A California Title IVC Project, Mind's Eye, helped me make a vital connection between reading and visualization.

From this influx of new information comes insight into both the problems and the solutions for many students. They are simply not visualizing from what they read. Even when they can read each word, they do not get the visual image that the author intended. To help them increase their understanding and discover the joy of reading, we must help our students develop the skills of visualization.

Visualization: the Missing Link in the Reading Chain

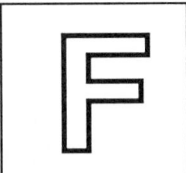For those of us who read well and with pleasure, a crucial point may be hard to believe: students who do not read well or who read without pleasure are probably not getting a mental image of what is happening in the stories they read. And, without the ability to visualize and bring forth images, they will remain as they are, weak readers.

This book offers a sequential program to help your students develop and use the skill of visualization to greatly expand the quality and quantity of their reading. The methods and lessons found here will help your students first to image, and then to use that imaging skill in their daily reading.

Recent research into the functioning of the two halves, or hemispheres, of the brain, supports this approach to reading. This research suggests that for learning to be complete, with long-term effects, both sides of the brain need to be involved. Visualizing is one path to right brain processing, while written words in our system of alphabetic symbols are often a path to the left.

It is the right brain that 'sees' the meaning. It makes sense of the rote process. It is the right brain that, after all the drudgery, has the "Aha!" experience. According to Bob Samples, Einstein was aware of this dual nature of the brain. He called the one half his faithful servant, as it did all the listing, compiling, and calculating. But it was the other half of his brain that fit all the pieces together to come up with a whole that was greater than the sum of the parts.

For a fully functional brain, it is very important that the two hemispheres communicate.

As we work with children in developing their capacity for visualization, we also help them establish the link between the brain hemispheres. It is essential to lead the students to make a connection from the images to language.

This linking of left and right brain can be done through writing, oral expression, drawing, and many other means. In this book I use the word *grounding* to signify that process of connection between the two hemispheres. After every visualization exercise, the students are given a way to ground their images. They are given the opportunity to represent something of what they saw on paper.

An extra benefit, that I did not anticipate when I conceived this program, is that the students' writing improves tremendously. If you get into the habit of giving time for visualizing before writing, your students have something of interest and depth to write.

Teachers in my county who have used this program on a trial basis have borne out my own experience, finding that many low readers show large gains in comprehension when measured on standardized reading tests, and nearly all students involved in the program increase the quantity of their independent reading many times over.

HOW TO USE THIS MANUAL

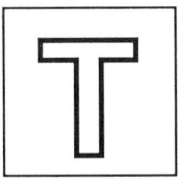he remainder of this book provides you with complete, step-by-step lesson plans. These plans will enable you to implement a complete visualization/literature reading program that is designed to help students to read and comprehend at their highest levels. Chapters 2 through 11 teach students to create rich, detailed visual images, and then use that skill as they read. When students are regularly visualizing as they read, they will be ready for the literature section.

Chapters 12 through 15 show how to get students reading good children's literature with understanding and enjoyment. Included are a management system and suggestions for greatly expanding time spent on good reading choices.

This manual can be used either as a basis for an entire reading program, or as a supplement to your existing reading program.

Used as a Supplement to Other Reading Programs
Although you may wish to implement only the visualization segment, or only the literature segment, I find that they work best when used together, because most students enjoy their reading so much more once they are creating vivid pictures.

❖ **How to Use This Manual**

The Overview provides a clear idea of the exact times needed each day, as well as a description of the activity of each chapter and an explanation of the purpose of that activity. The visualization chapters are strictly sequential. Students will not have the skills to do the more complex activities until they have been taken through the earlier exercises. Activities in each chapter build upon the skills developed in the preceding chapter. By the time students have completed the activities in Chapters 2 through 11, they should be visualizing richly as they read, and their comprehension and their enjoyment should have greatly expanded.

The literature section, which includes a sound management plan, consists of three main segments:
1. a daily time for classroom reading and tracking of children's literature, with each student self-selecting reading material of value,
2. a daily homework program of self-selected literature, and
3. daily oral reading of quality children's literature by the teacher. The program is further enriched by work with higher level questioning techniques to improve reading comprehension.

This plan will hold students accountable for their reading, while allowing them to read material suited to their own interests and abilities. Students will be reading, or being read to, for a total of over an hour a day, long enough to make a difference in their reading ability and enthusiasm. Nothing increases reading ability and reading enjoyment like extended time spent reading stimulating books. Students should become their own lifelong teachers as they learn to use books for pleasure, for learning, and for pursuing new ideas.

Used as the Basis for Your Reading Program
On page 21 you will find a Plan for the School Year. This outlines how much time you might spend on each chapter in this manual during the course of a school year. I emphasize that this plan is flexible, and I encourage you to adapt it to meet your own particular needs. The outline is provided here to enable you to conceptualize how a visualization/literature program could fit into the available spaces in your year-long reading program.

I recommend that you do the chapters in the order they are presented, since the skills in each chapter build upon those developed in the preceding activity. The non-visualizing, non-reading student, whom you most want this reading program to affect, will be the one who gets lost if you skip around.

There is an exception to this guideline: the Oral Reading, presented in Chapter 15, can and should be started on the first day of school and continued daily throughout the school year.

What About Skill Building?
The teaching of basic skills such as skimming, summarizing, and library skills is not covered in this manual because those are well handled in most basic reading programs. The purpose of this book is to teach visualization to increase understanding and comprehension and to develop enthusiastic, able readers.

Overview

Chapter 1: Preparation

Description
Teacher explains the process of visualizing and the reasons for it, setting guidelines and putting students at ease.

Purpose
To introduce students to visualization and help them understand its purpose and process.

Scheduling
Time needed: 15-30 minutes
Number of lessons: One.

Chapter 2: I Remember Mama

Description
Blindfolded, students will be given a sensory stimulus to elicit memories of similar sensations.

Purpose
To recall memories as a first path to imaging and to link right and left brain by imaging and drawing. Recalling memories is a comfortable way to approach the development of visualization skills.

Scheduling
Time needed for each lesson: 45-50 minutes
Number of lessons: Five
Extended activities: For optional development.

Chapter 3: Listen My Children and You Shall See

Description
Blindfolded, students are to image familiar objects (trees, shapes, animals), and then to change their color, size, or position in space.

Purpose
To teach students to image familiar objects at will and to alter and move these objects in response to verbal directions.

Scheduling
Time needed for each lesson: 40-45 minutes
Number of lessons: Three
Extended activities: For optional development.

Chapter 4: Archetypes

Description
Blindfolded, students will be asked to image a common archetype (wicked witch, kind mother, handsome prince). Students will then direct these archetypes to speak and take action.

Purpose
To begin to image characters and 'hear' speech. These activities will prepare students to build a set of prediction skills based on what they know of a character's personality.

Scheduling
Time needed for each lesson: 45-50 minutes
Number of lessons: Three
Extended activities: For optional development.

Chapter 5: Characters and Settings

Description
Students will visualize while teacher reads descriptions of characters and settings. Movement and speech will also be directed.

Purpose
To teach students to create settings and characters from books and stories, so that these elements come to life in their own reading.

Scheduling
Time needed for each lesson: 30-45 minutes
Number of lessons: Five.

Chapter 6: Magic Journeys

Description
Students will be guided through an adventure in which they are the main characters. The teacher will develop the situation and then ask students to complete the Journey independently.

Purpose
To help students develop abilities to predict actions and provide solutions independently. This activity can have great impact on the quality of students' writing by giving them something meaningful to write about.

Scheduling
Time needed for each lesson: 45-50 minutes
Number of lessons: Three.
Extended activities: For optional development.

❖ Overview

Chapter 7: Create a Myth

Description
Students will be guided through a universal myth, up to the point of climax. They will then be given time to visualize a resolution and finish the myth.

Purpose
To extend work begun in Chapter Six to develop a sense of plot, working through conflict and resolution. Myths are used because the story line is so powerful that it draws the student to a clear and meaningful ending.

Scheduling
Time needed for each lesson: 60-70 minutes
Number of lessons: Three.

Chapter 8: Image While You Read

Description
Teachers guide small groups of students in reading. Then, each student describes in detail what he or she has visualized from that sentence. Later, students read a paragraph at a time, then a whole story. Always, the teacher asks for the images in detail.

Purpose
To transfer the skill of visualization to the printed word. Students develop the habit of making a detailed picture in their minds' eyes for everything they read. They develop images for characters, settings, and action.

Scheduling
Time needed for each lesson: 60-80 minutes
Number of lessons: Ten.

Chapter 9: What Turtle?

Description
The class reads a story aloud together. As each section is read, the teacher quizzes students verbally about the pictures they are creating to give life to the story.

Purpose
To reinforce further the skills of visualization while reading and to promote the habit of reading.

Scheduling
Time needed for each lesson: 30-40 minutes
Number of lessons: Two or three a week for two weeks. Then, one or two a week for several months, as needed.

Chapter 10: Imaging in Content Areas

Description
The techniques outlined in Chapter Nine will be repeated, this time using material out of the content areas.

Purpose
To teach students to use their visualizing skills to increase comprehension as they read in the content areas.

Scheduling
Time needed for each lesson: 30-45 minutes
Number of lessons: Five
(One daily for one week; then, one per week, as needed, scheduled in the content area time period.)

Chapter 11: Vocabulary Books

Description
The teacher will choose five related words that students are not likely to know. They will image one word a day and draw what they visualize. At week's end they will write one sentence, correctly using all the vocabulary words.

Purpose
To develop skills and strategies for comprehending new words encountered in independent reading. Students will play with the meaning of words and perceive new words as interesting puzzles.

Scheduling
Time needed for each lesson: 30-40 minutes
Number of lessons: One, plus suggestions for nine more to be created by the teacher.

Chapter 12: Comprehension

Description
Students will read a common material. The teacher will lead a whole-class or small-group discussion, using Hilda Taba's Levels of Questions.

Purpose
To improve reading comprehension through practice in high level thinking skills and to use literature in the practice.

Scheduling
Time needed for each lesson: 30-45 minutes
Number of lessons: One model for teacher-designed lessons. Schedule two in first week, then one per week for remaining weeks.

❖ Overview

Chapter 13: Reading and Sharing Books

Description
Students read independently self-selected books, 20 to 30 minutes daily. In the last 10 minutes of the period, students share what they have been reading, while the class and the teacher ask a few questions.

Purpose
To expose students to a large variety of books by sharing them with their peers and to generate excitement and enthusiasm for reading.

Scheduling
Time needed for each lesson: 30-45 minutes
Number of lessons: Daily for the rest of the year.

Chapter 14: Homework Program

Description
Students will read their own literature selections every evening. Grades will be based on the amount read and verified by a parent.

Purpose
To develop a habit of daily reading, thereby increasing reading skills and vocabularies through practice and exposure.

Scheduling
Time needed for each lesson: 30-60 minutes
Number of lessons: Four per week at home.

Chapter 15: Oral Reading

Description
Teacher will read daily to students for 15-20 minutes. Selections will be interesting, high quality, and a bit above the reading level of most of the class.

Purpose
To stimulate interest in books, increase vocabularies, provide models of correctly spoken language in a variety of styles, and motivate students to read more.

Scheduling
Time needed for each lesson: 15-20 minutes.
Number of Lessons: One daily, selected by the teacher, preferably for most of the year.

Plan for the School Year

This program can be used in conjunction with the best of whatever reading program you have been using, or whatever program your school district may require. Here is a suggested outline of when you might use the various parts of the program. In the time available each day when you are not involved in the activities from this program, you will be able to teach the parts of your current reading program that you have found valuable. In addition, with the recent surge of interest in literature-based curriculum ideas, you will soon have the opportunity to learn many exciting things to do with students who are reading good literature. Keep your eyes open for workshops and books that can take you farther in this area of teaching reading; the ideas are springing up faster than wildflowers in springtime.

Basic Development of Visualization

For the first week of school, or even the first two weeks, depending on your class or reading style, use your regular reading program. Use this time to train your students in classroom rules, routines, etc. Start daily Oral Reading (Chapter 15) for 20 minutes each day, and continue this throughout the school year. On the second or third week of school, start the visualization program.

WEEK ONE:	I Remember Mama (Chapter 2) daily for 45 minutes each day.
WEEK TWO:	Listen My Children (Chapter 3) for 3 days at 40 minutes each day.
WEEK THREE:	Archetypes (Chapter 4) for 3 days at 45 minutes each day.
WEEK FOUR:	Characterizations and Settings (Chapter 5) daily for 40 minutes each day.

✣ **Plan for the School Year**

    WEEK FIVE: Magic Journeys (Chapter 6) for 3 days at 45 minutes each day.

    WEEK SIX: Create a Myth (Chapter 7) for 3 days at 60 minutes each day.

    WEEK SEVEN: Image While You Read (Chapter 8) daily for 60 minutes each day.

    WEEK EIGHT: Image While You Read daily for 60 minutes each day.

    WEEK NINE: Start your daily silent Reading and Sharing Books (Chapter 13) for 30 minutes each day. Also start the Homework Program (Chapter 14). This takes no class time. Continue both for the remainder of the school year.

Your students will now be reading with rich visualization, and your classroom and homework reading programs will support and encourage growth in all areas of reading as the year unfolds.

Extension of Visualization:

    WEEK NINE: Include a 30 minute lesson from What Turtle? (Chapter 9) on one day of the week, and a lesson from Comprehension (Chapter 12) on another day.

    WEEK TEN: Include a Vocabulary Book (Chapter 11) for 30 minutes of each day.

    WEEK ELEVEN: Include a lesson from Imaging in Content Areas (Chapter 10) for 30 minutes one day, and develop an Enrichment Visualization from Chapters 2-7 on another day.

    WEEK TWELVE: Same as week nine.

    WEEK THIRTEEN: Same as week ten.

    WEEK FOURTEEN: Same as week eleven.

Continue this cycle for the rest of the year, or until you want to change it to better meet your students' needs. As you develop your own repertoire of exciting activities to do in the field of children's literature, you will want to have time for these innovations as well.

EVALUATION

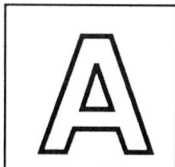s you evaluate your students' performance, keep in mind the true goals of this program. Primarily, the practice spent in learning to visualize should result in an increased reading ability and a great enthusiasm for reading. At the end of the first year of this program, I asked the parents of my students whether their children were reading more and liking it more than ever. All but one said yes. I counted the program a rousing success.

I hope that, as you evaluate your students' progress in reading, your first emphasis will not be on grades, but on assessing where they are in their abilities and enjoyment of reading, and what help you can provide to give them the boost that they need to continue improving.

But grades are a reality, and you will probably be expected to assign grades to students who have varying abilities and varying degrees of effort and involvement. If you abandon the easily graded comprehension dittos, then you may be wondering how you can possibly grade your students.

The answers to this question will be as different as each of you who reads this book. I can, however, give you some suggestions based on my own experience. These can serve as a springboard from which to create the kind of evaluation and grading system that will work for you in your particular situation.

❖ **Evaluation**

My evaluation system is based on the idea that effort and responsibility on the part of the student should be the basis for grades. No matter what their incoming reading levels, students can get an 'A' in my reading class. In so doing, those students must do a great amount of reading, and this constant practice will serve to improve reading comprehension greatly.

Early in the year, when the student may be reading below grade level and still making enough effort to reach the standards set for an 'A,' I make a notation on the report card that while the student is putting forth excellent effort and showing much improvement, the tested reading performance is still below grade level. I must, of course, give a formal reading survey to determine the truth of this statement before reporting it to the parents.

EVALUATION OF THE TWO STRANDS

1. The Visualization Exercises
In this strand your judgment of the students' efforts to complete grounding assignments will provide the basis for evaluating progress, if you are assigning grades.

When the student does what I have asked for, I give a grade of a check mark. When the student does more than I have asked for, I give this paper a plus mark. When the student does less than I have asked for, I give a grade of a minus mark. (If the student does nothing at all, that results in an 'F.') At the end of the quarter, I give all the pluses a weight of five points, all the checks a weight of three points, and all minuses a weight of one point. F's are zero. I then add the points and divide by the total of assignments, and translate the numbers into letter grades.

A great deal of what we do in the classroom, especially in visualization exercises, comes under the heading of practice and doesn't need to be carefully graded. To encourage students to experiment and take a chance on learning something new, we should not grade everything they do.

In place of formal grades, you might have your students keep a Visualization Exercises Folder containing all of their drawings and writing for the year. At the year's end, students may take their folders home with your confirming checkmark for orderly completion.

2. The Literature Strand

The evaluation system outlined in the last pages of Chapter 14 (Homework Program) is based upon the amount of time each student spends reading at home, a record that is verified by a parent signature each evening. As soon as the homework program is put into effect, probably in the eighth or ninth week of school, you will have a weekly grade for each of your students. These weekly grades are totaled at the end of each quarter. The students' Reading Record Folder, in which they list the books they have finished reading, also provides a basis for grading. I set a minimum number of books for each grading period except for the first period of the year. Students must read a certain number to earn an A, a B, or C. I keep the numbers within the reach of students who start the year as low reading achievers.

Putting It All Together

You now have two quarterly grades: one for Visualization Exercises, and one for Literature. How you combine these grades will depend on the extent to which each was emphasized in each grading period. Clearly, the Visualization grade will count for more in the first quarter, since the homework part of the Literature Program's grade isn't usually begun until eight or nine weeks into the quarter, when you are sure all of your students have learned to visualize.

How you use the suggestions in this chapter will depend on your own philosophy about the use and usefulness of grades and evaluation. In the final analysis, you will be able to evaluate your students' success to some extent by standardized testing. Extensive reading helps students become better readers, which is usually reflected in better grades. It is always helpful to give students some instruction and practice in test-taking tasks shortly before that experience rolls around. Students will be more relaxed and will do better if given some practice in test taking with clear instructions about strategies to use. Do not evaluate your whole program on these measures alone but also ask students and parents for feedback, in person and in surveys. Notice how you and your students feel about reading, measure and compare the quantity and quality of material read, and always keep in mind whether you are meeting your educational goals. Are the students reading more, with greater understanding and enjoyment? In this program I have found that they do.

SECTION I

VISUALIZATION

1 Preparation

Many a new project in each teacher's career has been abandoned in frustration. For a new project to be successfully implemented, both teacher and students must be well prepared.

FOR THE TEACHER

Be committed to developing the skills of visualization. Building a solid foundation of visualizing skills and learning to ground that visualization in symbols are two essential factors in this plan to bring your low-interest, low-achievement students into the pleasure and excitement of reading. Until these students can understand that pictures can be seen in the mind and be elicited by written language, they will see no point in struggling once again with those printed words that have been dull, dry, and painful for so long.

The first skill to help your students develop is that of visualization itself. Once this is well on its way, you can begin to transfer this ability to the printed word. For those who have found reading less than pleasant, you can then associate the imaging that they have been enjoying to the visualizing that they will soon be doing from the printed page.

DESCRIPTION
Teacher explains the process of visualization and the reasons for it, setting guidelines and putting students at ease.

PURPOSE
To introduce students to visualization and help them understand its purpose and process.

SCHEDULING
Time Needed: 15-30 minutes
Number of Lessons: One.

✤   Preparation

Have all materials ready.
It is important to distribute materials needed for the grounding exercise even before you begin the visualization work. This is because students need to begin grounding their images as soon as they open their eyes. Otherwise they will lose much of the energy that their imaging has generated.

What if a student "sees" nothing?
Some students protest that they do not "see" anything. Tell them to shut their eyes for a minute during the drawing period and imagine something you have read to them. If they still say they can't see anything, ask them to notice the color that they see with their eyes closed. Tell them to draw that. As they realize that you require an image, most will begin to look a little harder to get something interesting to draw with the rest of the class.

Tell your students: *Today we are going to start on a new program. It is based on new information about the left and right side of the brain and how it learns.*

We use the left side of our brains much of the time. But, the right side is the side that brings meaning to the information the left side has gathered. The right side gives us the "Aha!" experience. If we don't use the right side much, it gets weak.

So, in this program, you're going to work with that right side of the brain—to help you learn to make pictures in your mind's eye. And, when you can visualize those pictures in your mind's eyes, your reading will open up whole new worlds for you to experience.

You are going to start by doing something you don't usually do in the classroom. You are going to close your eyes—and keep them closed while we all work through part of a lesson.

Shut your eyes just for the count of three. Ready, one, two, three. Great. Now for the count of five. One, two, three, four, five. Very good. Now close them just until you see the color red, then open them. (As eyes open, you can say, "I see Carli saw red, Tom did, and Marcy, etc.) *Now shut your eyes long enough to see a pencil. It is a yellow school pencil. See if you can turn it red . . . . .* (For each dot, leave about one second of silence) *How about purple, a purple pencil . . . . .*

Now open your eyes. Show me with your hands how long your pencil was. Raise your hand if it was sharp. Dull? Not sharpened at all? Raise your hand if you didn't see a pencil. That's fine, too. We are going to be learning how to make clearer and clearer mental pictures.

Using your mind's eye is just like using a muscle. The more you use it, the stronger it will become. If you do not see anything clearly yet, you can pretend that you see something. As you pretend, your visualization 'muscle' will grow stronger.

Now you are ready to begin the first Journey. (If your introduction has been lengthy, wait until the next day to begin the Baby Powder Journey. If it has been brief, go right into the next chapter.)

2
I Remember Mama

DESCRIPTION
Blindfolded, students will be given a sensory stimulus to elicit memories of similar sensations.

PURPOSE
To recall memories as a first path to imaging and to link right and left brain by imaging and drawing. Recalling memories is a comfortable way to approach the development of visualization skills.

SCHEDULING
Time needed for each lesson: 45-50 minutes
Number of lessons: Five
Extended activities: For optional development.

RATIONALE
To help students begin to create the images that they need for meaningful reading, we begin by using their senses to recall strong memories.

As each student touches, smells, hears, and tastes the objects that you will present, memories should be unlocked. These memories come from the right brain in a total way, with all the senses in play. If students remember a dog, they may remember the touch of the dog's fur, his smell when wet, the feeling of the dog's tongue on their fingers, the sound of the dog barking, and perhaps even their feeling of loss after the dog was gone.

Because of this holistic function of the right brain, the following exercises continually stress use of all the senses. Notice that as you read each sample Journey, every sense is mentioned, even if it is far-fetched. When a sound is introduced, students are asked to see what color it is, what smell it has, how it would taste, and whether it would be hot or cold. Students are sensitive to different senses. For some, hearing might be the swiftest path to creating images. For others, it could be touch or smell.

BABY POWDER JOURNEY

PREPARATION
- Tell students that the purpose of this exercise is to increase their ability to see pictures with their mind's eyes when something is handed to them.
- Distribute paper, crayons, and blindfolds. Have the students set aside the paper and crayons, in a place very easy to access. Explain that the blindfolds are to help them concentrate on their own mind pictures, and to minimize the distraction that comes from vision. Tell them that you will be handing them certain objects during the activities and that their desire to open their eyes to see those objects will be more than mere will power can control. The blindfolds will help them remember.
- Have students remove jackets or sweaters if possible and roll up long sleeves and pants legs.
- Dim the lights as a signal to put on blindfolds.

RELAXATION
After the blindfolds are in place, but before the guided visualization begins, it is important to help your students relax their bodies and minds. A mind full of anticipation, worries, anger, frustration, and other tensions can easily interfere with concentration. When the students need a minute or so to shake off their busy thoughts and begin to tune you in, they easily miss a major part of each activity.

To provide for this eventuality, a relaxation exercise has been provided at the beginning of each activity. This will help to insure that, by the time you start the visualization section, the class will be ready for it. There are also some very delightful side benefits to this kind of exercise. Some studies suggest that when students relax before learning something new or before being tested, they learn, retain, and perform significantly better.

**MATERIALS NEEDED
For Each Student**
Unlined paper, crayons or oil pastels, blindfold, and a piece of cotton which has been tossed in a bag containing a sprinkling of baby powder. (Small black Halloween eye masks work well as blindfolds; put masking tape over the eye-holes, inside and out.)

♣ **I Remember Mama**

When blindfolds are in place, read the following:

Before we begin on our Journey today, I want you to take a minute to relax and clear your mind of other thoughts so that you will be able to focus completely on something that I am going to hand you.

When I say relax, I do not mean that you will lose your alertness. In our Western world we often think of 'alert' and 'relaxed' as opposites, but in many Eastern disciplines such as Judo, Karate, or Aikido, students try to bring the body to a state that is both totally relaxed and totally alert. Completely free of tension, but completely alert and ready for action. It is this kind of relaxation that our exercises are meant to effect in mind and body.

Now we are going to take some slow, deep breaths, imagining that, as we inhale, we can see and feel the oxygen going all through our bodies in our bloodstream. As we exhale, we can imagine the waste products from cells all over our body going out of our lungs and out of our mouths.

Take a deep, slow breath now, gradually filling your chest with all the air you can . . . (For each dot allow about one second of silence. If you will breathe along with your own instructions—not an easy thing to do—you will get the timing about right for your students.) *Now hold it . . . then slowly exhale, letting out all the old, stale air.*

Now this time breathe slowly into your stomach, filling your whole stomach with clean new air. Let your stomach stick way out to make room for all the air you need. . . . Hold it . . . then slowly, slowly exhale . . . This time, as you breathe in, first fill up your whole stomach, letting it stick out to hold all the air . . . then fill your chest too . . . see how much air you can hold . . . then very slowly let it all out.

Continue to breathe in that way, filling first the stomach, then the chest . . . hold it . . . slowly let all the air out . . . get it all out this time . . . then again, filling your stomach and then your chest, feeling the oxygen going all the way down to your knees and ankles and feet and toes. Then breathe slowly all the way out . . . let all that old air out. Then again, all the way in, all the way down your arms to your wrists and hands and fingernails . . . then slowly, all the way out. Get rid of it all. Again, all the way in, this time see the oxygen streaming to your brain, little oxygen scrub brushes cleaning your brain out and bringing it to life. . . . then all the way out . . . Now take one last deep breath, all the way in . . . . and all the way out . . . .

Now just pay attention to your normal breathing . . . . . See how your body feels . . . more relaxed than before . . . pay attention to how your brain feels . . . .

VISUALIZATION
In just a minute I am going to hand something to you. Do not try to guess what it is; that is not important. If you do think of what the object is, please do not call out its name. I want everyone to get a chance to experience this object.

When I give you your object, please hold it quietly in your hands. It will take me a little while to get around the room. Do not do anything with the object until I tell you. Now put your hands out in front of you and hold them together so that I can drop something in them. If you drop this object, do not remove your blindfold and look for it. Just raise your hand, and I will give you another. (Now you will hand out the baby-powdered cotton balls, saving the last few for those whom you suspect will have trouble keeping quiet about them.)

You probably all know what this might be, but now I want you to see what pictures you can get in your mind's eye. Not a picture of this object, but pictures or memories of other times you have felt this object in your hands. Now, keeping your mind's eye open to anything you might remember, please take the object in one hand and rub it on the back of your other hand . . . . .Rub it on your palm . . . . .Rub it between your fingers softly . . . . .then harder . . . . .Now change hands and do the same thing, first rubbing the back of your hand . . . . .then the palm . . . . and between the fingers gently . . . . .and then harder . . . .

Now hold the object in one hand and rub it on your forehead . . . . .on your cheeks . . . . .on your chin and neck . . . . .What color do you suppose this object is ? . . . . Smell it lightly . . . . .Where have you smelled that smell before? . . . . .If that smell were a color, what color would that smell be? . . . . .Now hold the object with your other hand . . . Bring it up on one ear . . . . Touch just the

♣ I Remember Mama

outside of your ear and notice what sound it makes........Notice what it feels like when you rub it on your ear........Try to make a different sound with it........Don't forget to keep your mind's eye open to memories of other times you have heard this sound or felt this feeling against your ear.......Try the other ear........Keep it just on the outside of your ear...Now rub it behind your ear.......

Now touch the back of your neck softly.......Now rub harder........Perhaps you remember a time when you felt this feeling on the back of your neck....Do you see a picture?...... (You don't want them to answer aloud, only to reflect. You may have to say this for the first few times you ask this kind of question.)

Now let's put this object on your arm.... move it up and down your arm.......Put the object on the outside of your elbow....and on the inside....Now do the same thing on your other arm........Don't forget your elbows, outside.....and inside.....

Now if you can, rub the object on one knee........Keep your mind's eye open for any pictures that come in from other times that you have felt this feeling, perhaps when you were very young. Now rub behind your knee........Now put this object on your other knee...... and behind it......
Now I am going to come around and collect the objects. Do not take off your blindfold yet. I do not want you to see the objects yet. I will show them to you later. If you look now, you will only be cheating yourself by limiting your imagination. Just hold the object quietly in both hands now. Hold them out in front of you, and I will pick them up. (Do this as quickly as you can, but do not get students to assist.)

GROUNDING

Not yet, but in just a minute I will ask you to take off the blindfolds. Not yet. But when I do, I want you to represent on your paper some of the pictures or memories that you just saw in your mind's eye. I do not want just a picture of what you think I handed you. The object itself might be a part of some of your images, especially if you made a guess about its color, but I want you to represent the memories that the object reminded you to see. Putting your memories down on paper will help you to remember more of what you saw, and will make it easier to see images the next time we do this. Do not worry about whether your picture looks great. Our purpose is not to make great art, but to remind you of the images you saw.

I will not be grading these drawings, although I will collect them. (With a hard-to-motivate or low achieving group, add: *All papers with drawings on them will receive an automatic 'A,' and any blank papers will get an 'F'*). *If you have any questions while you are drawing, just raise your hands and I will come to your desks. I do not want any talking until everyone has had the chance to get their images down on paper.*

Now, take off your blindfold and start drawing, with no talking please. Ready, begin.

During this drawing time, quickly create your own drawing; then walk around the room and talk to students briefly and quietly about their drawings. A few students who do not wish to share publicly may talk to you in private. Some visualizations can be very personal and inappropriate for public sharing.

This is also the time to help non-visualizers. If they say they are not drawing because they saw nothing, tell them to draw the nothing they saw. What color was it? What shape? They can also shut their eyes and look again, drawing what they see now. It is vital to the program's success that each student be required to draw. Those non-visualizers who are not urged to draw will have little reason to make the effort; those who keep drawing red or black for several days will get bored and begin thinking up something else to draw.

NOTES ON GROUNDING

Grounding provides the essential link between right and left brain, between imagery and symbol. It consists of some kind of physical representation of the image that was seen in the mind. It could be accomplished through drawing, writing, dancing, painting, sculpting, or singing, to list a few of the possibilities. For classroom purposes, I find that, at first, it is best not to use writing as the grounding medium, so that students will approach the visualizing process without any old hates or fears of the written word. Later in the program, when visualizing is established as a pleasant activity, I add writing as one of our grounding activities. You might experiment with other media later.

I draw along with my students, modeling simple, representational drawings. Sometimes I draw a picture that has only a color or shape motif. This way they can see that whatever they draw will be accepted. Remember, what they draw is not important. We are simply priming the pump of mental images.

SHARING
Call for volunteers to explain and share their drawings with the class. Remember, there is no 'right' or 'wrong' answer in visualizing. All drawings are acceptable. Be sure that students are not allowed to make fun of one another's work. I often share my simple drawings with the class; my sketchy artwork makes it all right for theirs to be simple, too.

It is often fun to count how many others saw a doctor's office, or of how many saw the color of the smell as green, or red, or blue, and so on.

NOTES ON SHARING
Sharing has several benefits:
1) Students enjoy sharing and appreciate hearing about their peers' ideas and images.
2) Students get a clearer idea of the wide range of acceptable drawings by seeing your drawing and those of their friends.
3) As Joseph Campbell points out in *Hero with a Thousand Faces*, there is an essential form and character to all great myths and journeys. In the final step in all journeys, the heroes share what they have learned or gained with the whole community. Only with this act of sharing does the journey complete its meaning. Inasmuch as these students are each asked to go inward to learn or gain something of value, it is a fitting conclusion that they share their riches with their classmates.

EVALUATION
Do not grade these efforts with letter grades, unless you have a group that is hard to motivate. Then you can tell your class that you will collect the drawings. Some youngsters need the push of knowing that they must make an effort, and these are often the very ones who have given up on reading, and whom we want most to motivate. You might even guarantee an automatic 'A' for all legitimate efforts. I have found this to be highly motivational for the student who usually gets a 'D' or an 'F' in reading.

A CANDY CANE JOURNEY

PREPARATION
- Remind students that the purpose of this Journey is not to guess what you hand them, but to let the object help them see pictures and recall times when they have experienced similar objects. The more pictures they can generate, the better.
- Distribute paper, crayons, and blindfolds, and have students put paper and crayons in an easily accessible place.
- Remind students that if they drop the object you will give them later, they are not to take off blindfolds and look for it, but raise their hands for assistance.
- Dim lights as a signal to put on blindfolds.
- Remind students that the first part of the Journey will be for relaxation, to clear their minds of outside thoughts or concerns and to help them focus on today's activity.

MATERIALS NEEDED
For Each Student
Unlined paper, crayon, blindfold, and an unwrapped candy cane.

RELAXATION
Please put your feet flat on the floor . . . . Shake out your shoulders . . and your arms . . . . . your hands and fingers . . . .and put your hands quietly on your desk top . . . . Please pay attention to your breathing; don't change it, just notice how it is going . . . . notice if you are breathing into your chest or into your stomach . . . . Are you breathing through your nose or through your mouth? . . . . Feel the air go in . . . and out . . . . .

All of us carry a certain amount of tension all of the time. In this exercise we want to lower that tension as much as we can, because it can keep our bodies from doing their best jobs for us. You have been watching and noticing your breathing; now I want you to notice the level of tension in your muscles . . . . Are they tense or relaxed? . . . . . . Maybe you have a lot of tension today . . . Sometimes, when we are worried or tired, we hold more tension than usual . . . Whatever you are feeling is just fine for you at this minute . . . Perhaps you don't feel very much tension today . . . Just notice what your level is.

. . . . in your feet . . . . . your legs . . . . . your shoulders . . . . . just notice if they are tense or relaxed . . . . .

I want you to call the level of tension that you have right now in your body a tension level of 5. Think of a dial that is your own tension control dial. Now it is set at 5. That is right in the middle. This dial can go up to 10 and down to zero. Right now your dial is set on 5.

Now I want you to turn the dial up to 6. . . You feel a little more tension than before . . . . . Turn it up to 7 . . . . . Up to 8 . . . . . Now let it slip back to 7 . . . . . back to 6 . . . . . back to 5 . . . . . This is where you started.

Now turn it up again, more tension . . . up to 6 . . . 7 . . . 8 . . . now up to 9 . . . . Then let it slide down to 8 . . . 7 . . . 6 . . . 5 . . . down to 4 . . . . . down to 3 . . . . Now go back up to 4 . . . . . and then to 5 . . . . Let's go up just a little again to 6 . . and 7 . . . then back down to 6 . . . 5 . . . 4 . . . 3 . . . down even more to 2 . . . . . then let it go down as far as you wish . . . . . Keeping the dial at this low level, notice your breathing now . . . See if there is any difference in how you are breathing now . . . . Now put the dial wherever you would like it to be . . . you can stay at zero if you like, very relaxed and alert . . . . . or you can put it on another setting . . . . .

VISUALIZATION

Today on our Journey, I am going to hand you something. Without changing the setting on your tension control dial, hold out both of your hands, and I will drop something in them. Remember, it is not important to guess what it is; you will be looking for memories of times when you felt something similar. If you happen to guess what the object is, please do not call out the name. I want everyone to have a chance to be surprised by it. (Hand out an unwrapped candy cane to each student.) *As I hand you today's object, please hold it quietly until I give you instructions.*

Hold the object in one hand, and gently tap it on your desk top . . . . Stop. Now listen for the color of the sound that it makes as you lightly begin tapping again . . . . Tap lightly, but quickly . . . . . Stop. Does this sound remind you of something?

Tap more slowly this time . . . . and stop. Now hold it in the palm of your other hand and tap it with the fingernails of your free hand . . . . . Keep your imagination open for any pictures that you are reminded of . . . . Now pinch it lightly and feel it with both hands . . . . . Turn the object around and explore it all over . . . . . What do you notice about its surface? . . . . . Have you felt something like this before?

Now bring the object up to one ear, and again tap it with your fingernails and listen to the sounds . . . . Now scratch on it . . . . What does this sound make you think of? . . . . . Now try the other ear, tapping it . . . . and scratching it . . . . Now hold it under your nose and smell . . . . When have you smelled something like this before? . . . . . Where were you when you smelled it? . . . . Now stick out your tongue and lick it . . . . . Notice the color of the taste as it touches your tongue . . . . . Lick it again, but don't put it inside your mouth just yet . . . . Now tap it softly against your top teeth . . . . tap it gently against your bottom teeth . . . . . What other times have you heard this sound? . . . . .

Now, using your top and bottom teeth, bite off the tiniest piece that you can possibly manage . . . Hold that piece in your mouth until it melts . . . . . (If you do this too, you will have the best sense of the time it will take) . . . Now even if the tiny piece isn't melted, chew and swallow it . . . . Now, again paying attention to the sounds you make, bite off a piece a little bigger and chew and swallow it as fast as you can . . . . Listen to the sounds . . . . . What do they remind you of? . . . . Notice the color of this taste as it goes down your throat . . . . Now you may eat the rest of this object if you like, quickly or slowly. I will give you one minute.

(After one minute has passed) *If you are not finished, you may either put the rest of it in your mouth or in your desk. I don't want anyone to look at this object until we have finished our pictures, so please put it in your desk now.*

GROUNDING
In just a minute, not yet, I will ask you to remove your blindfolds and draw any of the pictures that you saw. Your pictures can show the colors that you saw, or the memories that you had. They could even be pictures of designs or patterns that you made up. Remember, I am not asking for pictures of what you think

the object was. I want pictures of things it reminded you of. If you have any questions, please raise your hand, and I will come to your desk. Do not talk or whisper. I want everyone to concentrate on the drawing until all work is finished. Ready, take off the blindfolds and begin.

While the students are drawing, make your own picture and then circulate. Quietly ask for some of the more reluctant sharers to tell you a little about their pictures, and encourage the non-visualizers and non-drawers.

SHARING
Ask for volunteers to tell about their pictures and their memories. You might share yours. Let students notice where their pictures and memories are similar to their classmates. Remember, this is always a voluntary activity, as some visualizations may be very personal.

EVALUATION
Letter grades are not given to this activity, but do collect the drawings so that students know that you care.

ICE CUBE JOURNEY

PREPARATION
- Remind students of the purpose of the Journey.
- Distribute paper, crayons, blindfolds, and paper towels. Have them put the paper, crayons, and paper towel in their desks.
- Remind students to raise their hands if they drop the object, and not to take off blindfolds and search for it.
- Have students take off jackets and sweaters, and roll up sleeves and pants legs as far as possible. If they are willing, they can also take off their shoes and socks. I make this optional.
- Dim lights as a signal to put on blindfolds.

RELAXATION
Put your feet flat on the floor and your hands on your desk tops . . . . . We are going to take a few minutes to get relaxed before I hand you today's object. Wiggle your shoulders around a little to get out the kinks . . . . Now stop and put your hands gently on your desk top . . . . . and let's take five deep breaths together . . . . . I want you to breathe first into your stomach, then into your chest, letting them both fill up with air . . . and hold it . . . and slowly exhale, all the way out . . . . . All the way in, the oxygen goes down to your feet and toes . . . . . hold it . . . then breathe slowly all the way out. All that old stale air goes out of your body, out of your mouth. Again, all the way in . . . oxygen goes up into your brain, cleaning it out, getting it ready to remember . . . . . and all the way out . . . . . One more time, all the way in, fresh oxygen bringing in energy . . . . . then exhale slowly, all the way out . . . . . and again, all the way in . . . . . and let all the air out . . . . . .

Now I want you to tense all the muscles in your feet and legs, not the rest of you, just your feet and legs . . . . . make them as tight as you can . . . tighter still . . . now slowly let them relax . . . Now tense only your right foot and leg . . . Don't tense the left one, just the right foot and leg . . . . . tighter . . . . . Now let it slowly go . . . . . Now the left

MATERIALS NEEDED
For Each Student
Unlined paper, crayons, blindfold, a large ice cube, and a paper towel.

For The Teacher
Several extra ice cubes to replace those that are dropped or disappear in the dark.

✤ I Remember Mama

foot and leg . . . Don't let the right leg get tense, just the left one . . . . . tighter . . . . . and let go . . . . . .

Now we are going to tense both hands and arms, all the way up into your shoulders . . . . . Tense them both at once, not your legs or your faces, just your hands and arms . . . . . tighter, tighter . . . . . and let go . . . . . This time tense only your right hand and arm and shoulder. Tense your fist, your wrist, your elbow, your shoulder . . . . . Don't let the left side get tense; don't let your legs get tense, just your right arm tighter . . . tighter . . . . and then let go . . . . Now your left fist, your wrist, your arm, and elbow, your shoulder . . . . . Don't let anything else get tight, just the left fist, arm, and shoulder, tighter . . . tighter . . . and then let go . . . . .

Now tense your head and neck and face . . . . . your eyes, ears, nose, mouth, chin, cheeks, jaw, tighten up . . . tighter . . . and tighter . . . and then let go . . . . Let's take one more deep breath . . . all the way in . . . . and all the way out . . . .

VISUALIZATION

Please turn in your seat now so that you can hold your hands out in front of you but not over your desk top. What I am going to hand you today could get your desk top messy, so I want your hands out in front of you, over the floor, not over your desk. Please keep your hands out together, and I will put something in them. Do not guess what this object is; just look in your mind's eye for any pictures that this object may remind you of. If you know what the object is, please do not call out its name. I want all students to get a chance to feel it themselves. (Hand one large ice cube to each student.)

Now hold this object in just one hand . . . . . rub it on the back of your other hand . . . . Now rub it on your arm, up and down . . . outside and inside . . . . . Change hands and just hold it quietly . . . Notice how it feels there in your hand . . . When have you felt this sensation before? . . . . . Now rub it on the back of your other hand . . . . Now on the other arm . . . up and down . . Now hold the object in both hands at once . . . . . Hold it in just one hand and touch it to your cheek . . . . the other cheek . . . . Now with your lips closed, put the object on your mouth . . . . move it to a different part of the outside of your mouth . . . . . Now open your mouth and gently tap it on your top teeth . . . . . gently on your bottom teeth . . . . . touch your tongue to it . . . . .

Notice if you are reminded of memories of other times you have felt that sensation..... Now smell it..... What color does it smell like?..... Touch this object to the tip of your nose........

Now switch hands again, and touch the object to your knee if you can....... Put it at the back of your knee..... Slide it down your leg, and if you took off your shoes earlier, put the object on the top of your foot........ and on the bottom..... Notice if you are seeing other times that your foot felt like this........

Now hold the object in both hands again, off to the side of your desk, and I will pick it up. Do not remove your blindfolds; I will show you what you have been holding after you have finished the pictures. (Pick up the ice cubes.)

GROUNDING
Not yet, but in just a minute, I will ask you to remove your blindfolds. Do not take them off yet. When you do, you will probably need to wipe off the top of your desk with the paper towel. Then please draw something of what you saw or felt during the Journey. Do not draw a picture of what you think it was. Just represent anything you remember about other times you felt something like today's object. If you didn't see any memories, then pick a color that the object reminded you of and put that color on your paper. Or draw some shapes that the object felt like. If you have a question, please raise your hand, and I will come to your desk. No talking, please, until the drawings are done. Ready, take off your blindfolds and begin.

As the students clean up and draw, you can circulate among them and talk to those who have not been sharing with the class. Also encourage those who are not yet seeing or drawing.

SHARING
Ask for volunteers to share drawings or memories. Some may be willing to tell what they remembered, but not to show the picture. Anything they share is fine. Don't forget to share yours.

EVALUATION
Collect papers but do not grade.

✤ I Remember Mama

A CHIME JOURNEY

MATERIALS NEEDED
For Each Student
Unlined paper, crayons, and blindfold.

For The Teacher
A chime, one with a pleasant, strong sound. If nothing else is available, try a wind chime.

PREPARATION
- Remind students that the purpose of this exercise is to create pictures in their minds' eyes, and that there will be a relaxation time before the Journey begins.
- Distribute paper, crayons, and blindfolds.
- Dim the lights as a signal to put on blindfolds.

RELAXATION
Please put your feet flat on the floor . . . . . Shake out your shoulders . . . . . . Shake out your elbows . . . . . . your wrists . . . . . . your hands and fingers . . . . . . Now lightly rest your hands on your desk top.

Sit up straight and relaxed, using your center of gravity to do the work of holding yourself upright . . . take a moment to find that center . . . . . Then let's take five deep breaths, all the way in . . . filling your stomach and then your chest . . . . . and all the way out . . . getting rid of all the old air . . . . . and all the way in . . . . and all the way out . . . . All the way in . . . and all the way out . . . . Again, all the way in . . . . and all the way out . . . . And once more, all the way in . . . . and all the way out . . . .

Now you are going to climb up into your own brain. Imagine that you are walking down a corridor in the middle of your brain . . . . . There are doors on either side . . . . . There is a door marked "vision" . . . one that is marked "taste" . . . Here's one that is marked "smell" . . . but you are looking for the one that is marked "hearing" . . . . . There it is, you can make out the letters H - E - A - R - I - N - G. Open that door and walk in . . . . . You are now inside the hearing control center in your brain . . . . You notice that it is not as clean and neat as it could be . . . . . You see dust and cobwebs . . . . . With your magic wand, you produce a feather duster, a broom, a mop,

46

and a bucket of soapy water. You go to work cleaning up this room. You dust . . . . . you sweep . . . . . you mop . . . . . you straighten up . . . . . until the room is so clean that it fairly sparkles . . . . .

Now you notice two doors at the far end of the room . . . . . One door is marked "to the left ear," and the other is marked "to the right ear," Open these doors, and see that these are the corridors that lead the sound from your ear to the hearing control center in your brain . . . You notice that the corridors are pretty messy, lots of dust and dirt and cobwebs . . . . . You take your duster, your broom, and your bucket and mop into the corridor marked "to the left ear," and you scrub and rub and dust and mop until it is spotless . . . . Then you go back into the main room and open the door marked "to the right ear," and you go into that corridor as well . . . . . and clean and polish and rub and scrub until all the dirt is gone . . . . Now you go back into the main room. You open both the doors that lead to your ears, and you brace them so that they will stay all the way open. Now the sounds can easily travel from your ears down the corridors to this hearing control center . . . You take a last look around to see that everything is neat and clean and in its place, and that the doors to your ears are wide open . . . . . Then you leave the room and shut the big door behind you.

You walk back down the main corridor of your brain . . . . . past the doors marked "vision" and "smell" and "taste." You climb down out of your brain and back into your seat in this room . . . . .

VISUALIZATION
On your Journey today, I will not hand you anything. Today you will be listening. You will be listening to a sound that I will make. That is one reason we spent time cleaning out your brain's hearing center.

Don't try to guess what I am using to make the sound. Just as in other Journeys, you will try to see memories of other times. You will also let the sound create patterns and colors in your mind's eye.

First, as I move around the room and make this sound, I want you to get any pictures or memories of times when you have heard a sound like this. It may have been in a movie or on television. It may have been something you heard in person. Let the sound travel down the corridors in your brain, and see what pictures it brings. (Move to five or six places in the room, each time striking the chime and letting it ring until the sound has completely stopped.)

I am going to make that sound a few more times. As I do, concentrate on colors. What color do you think this sound is most like? You might even see more than one color. What color is this sound like? (Repeat striking the chime just as before.)

This time, as I make the sound, try to see the pattern it makes as it moves through the air. Does it travel in straight lines, or in circles? Does it move in a zigzag or a curve, or does it make some other pattern? (Strike the chime as before, two times.) . . . . *Is this pattern the same or different? (This time strike it rapidly three times.) How did that sound move through the air? What pattern did it make that time?* (Again strike it rapidly three times. Pause, then strike it three more times. Pause again, and strike it three times once again.)

Here is a different pattern. What color do you see now and what pattern do you see as this sound moves through the air? (Strike the chime, and after two or three seconds, stop the sound by touching it with part of your body. Repeat this sound.) *Is this color the same as the others, or different? What is the pattern like as it travels across the room?* (Repeat the process again, damping the sound. Do it five or six times.)

Now I am going to make the same sounds that I did the first time. As I do, you can image anything you wish. You might see memories of other times you heard these sounds, or you might see colors and patterns as the sounds move through space and cross the room to your ear. (Make the sounds as you did the first time, being sure to vary the volume by striking sometimes softly and sometimes very hard. Leave a ten-second silence after the last chime.)

GROUNDING
In just a minute, not yet, but in a minute, I will ask you to take off your blindfold and draw anything you saw. If you saw memories of other times you have heard the sound, you could represent those memories. The drawing doesn't have to look like what you really saw; it should just help you to remember the scene. If you

didn't have any memories of this kind of sound, draw the patterns or colors that you saw. If you have any questions, please raise your hand, and I will come to your desk. I do not want you to talk out loud until all of the drawings are finished. Then we will share our pictures, and I will show you how I made today's sound. Ready, remove the blindfolds and, without talking, begin.

While the students draw, make your own picture and then circulate, asking students to quietly tell you a little about what they are drawing, especially encouraging the non-drawers.

SHARING
Ask for volunteers to show and tell about their pictures. Notice similarities and differences, affirming that all responses are correct.

EVALUATION
These efforts will not be given letter grades, but you should collect the drawings so that the students know you are concerned that they do their work. Automatic grades of 'A' could be given as a motivator to low self-esteem readers.

❖ I Remember Mama

PINECONE JOURNEY

MATERIALS NEEDED
For Each Student
Crayons, blindfold, and a pinecone. (If pinecones are unavailable, sprigs of pine needles, sage, or bay leaves can be substituted.)

PREPARATION
- Remind students of the purpose of today's Journey: to open the mind's eye to memory pictures.
- Have students take off jackets and sweaters, and roll up sleeves and pant legs, if possible.
- Remind them that if they drop the object, they should not remove blindfolds, but raise their hands, and you will assist them.
- Distribute crayons, paper, and blindfolds. Have students fold the paper into fourths and then open it up again.
- Dim lights as a signal to put on blindfolds.

RELAXATION
Please put your feet flat on the floor . . . Shake out your shoulders . . . . . your head . . . . . your arms . . . . . . your hands and fingers . . . . Now place your hands gently on your desk top . . . . . and sit up straight and relaxed.

Imagine that a string is attached to the exact center of the top of your head, and that it is gently tugging your head upward into perfect balance on the top of your spinal cord . . . . . very gently tugging your head into perfect balance . . . . .

Now, in your mind's eye, take a look at your spinal column. It is made up of separate little bones that are stacked on top of each other like a very tall stack of blocks. In reality, between each of the little blocks called vertebra is a little cushion that keeps the bones from rubbing against each other when you move. Today we are going to imagine that each cushion is actually a small golden bubble . . . See the bones in your spinal column . . . . the vertebra each held apart from the next by a soft, golden bubble . . . . . . The bubbles don't force the bones apart, they cushion and protect them from each other . . . .

You can feel the golden bubbles, lifting each vertebra, adding just a tiny bit to your height as you sit in your chair . . . . .We are going to take five deep breaths now, and as we do, I would like you to imagine that some of the air you breathe is going to fill those little golden bubbles. Don't fill them too full; you don't want to make your back uncomfortable. Fill them just so they support and cushion your vertebra like little golden pillows.

Breathe all the way in . . . and feel the golden bubbles expand gently to lift and separate each vertebra . . . . . and all the way out . . . . the bubbles get a little smaller, but they still protect each little bone . . Breathe all the way in . . . . . the golden bubbles expanding . . . . and all the way out . . . . And all the way in . . . little golden cushions all up and down your back . . . . .and all the way out . . . . and all the way in . . . golden bubbles lift each vertebrae . . .and all the way out . . . . and once more, all the way in, feeling the golden bubbles gently expand . . . and all the way out . . . .

VISUALIZATION
Now, please put your hands together and hold them over your desk so that I can put something in them. When you get today's object, hold it quietly until I give you some instructions. Remember, it is not important to guess what the object is; it is your job today to see the memories the object brings to your mind's eye. Perhaps the object will smell like something you have smelled before. Maybe the sounds it makes will remind you of another place you have been, or of sounds you have heard somewhere else. If you guess what the object itself is, please do not call out its name. I want everyone to have the chance to encounter this object without any preconceived ideas.

Be very gentle with today's object. If you squeeze it tightly, it will break. If it gets damaged, you may have trouble following my instructions. If you drop the object on the floor, be sure to raise your hand and let me recover it. Do not remove your blindfold, or try to find it yourself. (Put a pinecone in each student's hands, saving the last ones for students most likely to have trouble keeping quiet about the nature of the object.)

Now hold this object with the fingers of one hand and lightly brush it on the back of your other hand . . . . now brush it on your palm and fingers . . . . keep your mind's eye open for other times that you have felt this sensation . .

I Remember Mama

...... Now brush your wrist....... and the inside of your arm..... and the outside of your arm........ Hold the object with the fingers of the other hand... and again brush it lightly against the back of your empty hand...... and against your palm and fingers ...... your wrist...... your inner arm...... your outer arm......

Now lightly rub this object on the outside of your legs as far up as you can go........ the inside...... and on your knees........

Now, keeping the object in your hand, lightly, so that it won't break, poke your arm and your empty hand with the end of this object........ See if you have felt this kind of a poke sometime before........ What color are the pokes?...

Now change hands again and bring the object up to your hair. Gently run it across your hair, noticing the sound it makes........ against the front of your neck........ your chin........your cheeks........ your forehead........ Now bring it right under your nose and gently smell.....Let yourself remember any other times you have smelled this smell........ Now turn it over and take an even deeper smell..... (If you are using leaves instead of the pine cone, you can have them break a leaf to intensify the smell, but be careful of the bay leaf; a deep whiff can cause a headache.) *Pay attention to the color of the smell as it travels into your nose and down into your lungs........ Does it stay the same color all the way down, or does it change as it travels along?.........Now move this object to one ear, and make some kind of sound against your ear........ notice if you have heard this sound somewhere before...... Now make a different kind of sound........ What does that remind you of?...... What color does the sound seem to be?....... Now try the other ear, making one kind of sound... listen carefully........ and make another kind of sound... what color is this sound? Is it a hot or a cold sound?..... Now bring the object to your mouth and gently touch your lips.....Have you ever eaten anything that felt like this on your lips?.....*

Now hold the object in both of your hands. I am going to pick it up from you. Later I will show you what it really looks like; for now, please be quiet and wait until I have picked them all up.

GROUNDING
Please keep your blindfold on. There are eight squares on your paper; four on the front and four on the back. In just a minute I will ask you to take off your blindfolds. Not yet. When I do ask you to remove them, I will want you to draw a small picture in each square, one for each memory or picture that today's object brought to mind. Besides putting down your pictures, you can represent sounds and smells that you remembered. If you don't have eight different pictures, put down as many as you do have. If you have any questions, please raise your hand and I will come to your desk. I want you to use your energy to quickly represent what you have imagined. If you waste time, you could forget what you saw in your mind's eye, so please do not talk or whisper. Ready, take off the blindfolds and begin. Start drawing right away.

As the students begin to draw, you can create your own picture, and then walk around, encouraging any who are not yet visualizing or drawing. Urge non-visualizing students to draw something.

They may have seen red, or black, or yellow spots; they should draw whatever they saw. They will begin to see something more interesting before long.

SHARING
Call for volunteers to explain and share their pictures. Also, share yours. Continue to accept and praise all efforts. Notice similar pictures, and contrast colors and pictures.

EVALUATION
This work will be collected, but not graded except as noted in the previous Journeys.

EXTENDED ACTIVITIES

These ideas for other Visualization Journeys can be developed now, or at your discretion, any time later in the year. The following guidelines will enable you to take the students on stimulating and pleasant Journeys.

- Repeat the relaxation exercises using one of the models I have provided for you. Select the one most appropriate to the Journey you have chosen.
- Write out your script beforehand, rather than make it up as you go along. At first thought you might expect that it would be fairly simple to invent changes in shapes and colors extempore, but it is very easy to forget some of the important elements you want to include.
- Follow the outline of a similar Journey that I have provided. For instance, to write a Hershey's Kiss Journey, simply alter the Candy Cane Journey to fit the slightly different nature of the candy.
- After I write out a Journey, I often tape myself reading with what seems like the right timing. Then I shut my eyes and listen to the tape, experiencing the Journey as my students will. If necessary, I can then adjust the timing or instructions.

MATERIALS NEEDED
For Each Student
Hershey's Kiss, lemon drops, several pieces of popcorn, peanut brittle, finger jello, a lifesaver, a piece of mild cheese, a carrot slice, an orange slice with rind, or a quarter of a lemon.

MEMORY JOURNEYS INVOLVING TASTE

Use the general format that you find in the Candy Cane Journey.

MEMORY JOURNEYS INVOLVING TOUCH

Use the general format that you find in the Ice Cube Journey. You can use the same relaxation and grounding exercises, or pick another that you enjoy.

MATERIALS NEEDED
For Each Student
Cotton, sandpaper, stones (smooth or rough), a soft stuffed animal, a metal bar (like a playground bar), a bunch of leaves, or softened clay.

MEMORY JOURNEYS INVOLVING HEARING

Use the same general format that you find in the Chime Journey.

MATERIALS NEEDED
For Each Student
An assortment of noisemakers, pipes, children's toys, song flutes, Halloween clickers, poker chips, beans in a paper cup, or a handful of wrinkled tissue paper.

For The Teacher
A timpani, a flute, a piano, good tones from any instrument (a violin, a tuba, a clarinet, etc.), a basketball, an electric mixer, an alarm clock bell, a xylophone, or a gong.

MEMORY JOURNEYS INVOLVING SMELL

Use the general format you find in the Pinecone Journey. You can use the same relaxation and grounding exercises, or any others that you like.

MATERIALS NEEDED
For Each Student
Bay leaves, pine needle sprays, sprigs of sage, a clove of garlic, a piece of onion, a fragrant flower, a cinnamon stick, a mint leaf, eucalyptus pods or leaves, fresh rosemary, or drops of vanilla on cotton.

ADDITIONAL ACTIVITY
- Listen to the sound the object makes; if very soft, put it up to the ear.

3
Listen My Children and You Shall See

DESCRIPTION
Blindfolded, students are to image familiar objects (trees, shapes, animals), and then to change their color, size, or position in space.

PURPOSE
To teach students to image familiar objects at will and to alter and move these objects in response to verbal directions.

SCHEDULING
Time needed for each lesson: 40-45 minutes
Number of lessons: Three
Extended activities: For optional development.

MATERIALS NEEDED
For Each Student
Unlined paper, crayons, and blindfold.

RATIONALE
The skill that we develop here, that of imaging action, is an essential part of making reading come to life in the mind's eye. The printed page says much, but it does not specifically direct the reader to visualize it. Many students have not imaged as they read. We begin to change that by purposefully showing them how to create moving pictures and to alter them at will.

COLOR JOURNEY

PREPARATION
- Tell your students that today the journey will be a little different. This time you will be asking them to create moving pictures, as if they had a movie screen in their minds' eyes.
- Distribute unlined paper, crayons, and blindfolds.
- Dim the lights as a signal to put on blindfolds.

RELAXATION

Put your feet flat on the floor. Please sit up straight, in a relaxed manner. Shake out your shoulders a bit to get out the kinks . . . then settle, relaxed and alert, in an upright position . . . .

Imagine that a golden thread is attached to the exact center of the top of your head. Ever so gently, that golden thread is tugging your head upwards so that it is lightly balanced on your spinal column . . . .

I want you to imagine your spinal column as golden blocks, each one stacked perfectly on top of the other. Starting at the base of your spine, you can notice each one as you travel up . . . and up your back . . . . Each block is stacked carefully on top, of the other in perfect balance . . . . Not tense or straining, just perfectly balanced and straight . . . . They rest gently on each other . . . . And at the top, the golden thread is gently guiding the round ball of your head into a delicate and perfect balance.

Now, with the golden thread holding up your round head, your spinal column of golden blocks forms a perfectly straight line. See if you can feel the straightness of the line . . . not tense, just straight, relaxed, and perfectly straight . . . Now I want you to imagine a golden energy flowing down that line into your spinal column . . . . Let it flow gently down the perfectly straight line that we have made . . . . It is a golden energy that allows your body to relax . . . . Not slumping over, just completely relaxed, and at the same time, completely alert and alive . . . . Feel this golden energy flowing down the golden thread and down through your head and your spinal cord . . . . . . It fills your body with a sense of being ready.

VISUALIZATION

Now I would like you to begin to see the color red. In your mind's eye you see red, nothing but red . . . . In the center of all of this red, begin to notice a small blue circle . . . The blue circle grows bigger, and bigger . . . bigger, and bigger . . . . until all you can see is blue. Blue, blue, and more blue . . . . . Then in the middle of the blue, you see a small yellow square . . . The yellow square grows, and grows . . . A yellow square getting bigger and bigger . . . crowding out the blue until there is nothing left but yellow . . . . . Let the yellow get lighter in color . . . Now let it darken to the color of egg yolks. Let it become an egg yolk in the

♣ Listen My Children

middle of a fried egg . . . . . Let the egg yolk get bigger and bigger until it is so big . . . that it breaks open and begins to drip downward . . . As it drips downward a new color, green, appears behind it . . . . . bright green appears as the egg yolk drips away to the bottom of your vision . . . . . And right in the middle of this new green are three orange tennis balls bouncing up and down . . . You watch the orange tennis balls bounce . . . They get bigger . . . They both turn red . . . then purple . . . then blue . . . then two turn red and one turns green . . . one turns black with white stripes and the others are yellow . . . Now one is big and red and the others are small and white . . . One of the small white balls bounces away, out of sight, and the other one bounces inside of the big red ball. Now the small white one is in the middle of the big red one, so that they form two circles, one inside the others. The outside circle is red . . . the inside circle is white . . . . Leave the outer circle red and turn the inner one yellow . . . Leave the inner one yellow and turn the outer one dark blue . . . Leave the outer one dark blue, and make the inner circle light blue . . . Now make the outer circle red and the inner circle orange . . . and put a small yellow dot right in the center of them both. Let the yellow dot grow and grow until it covers both of the other circles . . . then fill your vision with nothing but yellow . . . sun yellow . . . Let it turn orange . . . then red . . . then purple . . . then blue . . . then green. . . . then yellow again. In the center of this sun-yellow field, put the most wonderful animal you have ever known in your life . . . . . See the animal there in the center of this yellow glow . . . Any animal you have known, or any you have ever heard about . . . . . Notice if your animal is doing anything . . . In some way let this animal know that you care for it . . . . . then say good-bye for now . . . . . Know that you have created this animal in your imagination, and you can return to visit it in this way any time you want. Finish your good-byes and come back to the classroom. Feel the floor beneath your feet and the chair that is supporting you. Do not remove you blindfolds yet.

GROUNDING

Not yet, but in just a minute, when I tell you to take off your blindfolds, I want you to draw anything that you saw clearly in your imaging. Draw more than one scene, and use both sides of the paper if you wish. If you have any questions, raise your hand, and I will come to your desk. Do not talk until the drawings are finished. Ready, remove the blindfolds and draw.

After you have finished your drawing, circulate around the room.

SHARING
Ask for volunteers as usual. Students especially like telling about the animal they saw.

EVALUATION
Merely collect the drawings so that students know you care whether or not they do the work.

THE APPLE TREE JOURNEY

PREPARATION
- Remind students that they will be seeing action as you talk, just as if there were a movie screen in their minds' eyes.
- Distribute paper, crayons, and blindfolds.
- Dim lights as a signal to put on blindfolds.

MATERIALS NEEDED
For Each Student
Unlined paper, crayons, and blindfold.

RELAXATION:
Please be sure that your feet are flat on the floor . . . and shake out your shoulders . . . . and now put your hands gently on your desk top and sit in an upright position . . . I want you to balance your weight on your spinal column . . . Gravity and balance should do most of the work of holding your body upright so that your muscles can be relaxed and at ease . . . . You are aiming for a state that is both alert and relaxed . . . peaceful and energized . . .

Today, we are going to breathe in some colors, in long slow breaths. First, imagine that you are breathing in purple air . . . . The purple air fills your lungs and chest and then travels out all the way to your fingers . . . . As you exhale, all the purple air leaves your body, back to your lungs and out of your mouth . . . . Breathe another deep breath of purple air. It travels down your arms to your fingers and down your stomach and legs into your toes . . . . As you exhale, it all flows back into your lungs and out of your mouth.

Next, breathe in some blue air . . . Slowly fill your lungs with blue air and watch it go down your arms into your fingers, and down your legs into your toes . . . . As you exhale, watch it go back up your legs into your lungs, back up your arms into your lungs, and out of your mouth into the air. Let's breathe the blue air once again . . . notice how it smells going in . . . and exhale . . . . Notice the blue air as it leaves your mouth and goes back into the room.

Now orange . . . send orange air into every part of your body, legs and feet and toes, shoulders and arms and fingers . . . then back out in an orange cloud. Now turn the cloud yellow and breathe it in . . . sending yellow to every part of your body, like sending sunshine . . . . Let it flow up your neck and into your head and brain . . . . And then exhale and let it all go back to your lungs and out of your mouth . . . .

Now just notice your normal breathing for a moment . . . .

VISUALIZATION

On our Journey today you find yourself in the middle of a large field where things can grow . . . . . In front of you is a freshly dug piece of rich earth . . . In your hand is a seed . . . It is an apple seed . . . You put the apple seed in the ground and water it . . . . . You can see it begin to grow . . . . . It is obviously a magic seed and will take just a minute to become a full-sized tree. Right now, watch it grow taller and taller . . . . . putting out more and more branches . . . . . Watch the leaves appear on those branches . . . Now the tree is taller than you are . . . Now it is as tall as your house . . . Now it is even taller . . . . Now blossoms start to appear all over the apple tree . . . hundreds and hundreds of blossoms . . . A gentle breeze comes along and the blossoms begin to float down from the tree and lie on the ground . . . . Where the blossoms were attached, you can see the tiny apples beginning to grow . . . They are green and very small . . . . . As you watch, they begin to grow larger and larger until they are as large as the apples you buy at the store . . . . Then they start to change color . . . first from green to yellow . . . then red streaks appear . . . and finally they are red all over . . . Look at this big green tree with hundreds and hundreds of round, ripe, red apples hanging from its branches . . . . .

Now, one at a time, not all at once, each apple turns into an orange . . . pop, pop, pop, pop, until every apple has become a fat, round, orange . . . . Now let each orange, one by one, turn into a banana. Pop, pop, pop, pop . . . . .

Nothing but bananas now . . . Step back and see this big green apple tree covered with bananas. Yellow bananas hanging from every branch. Now, all at once, the bananas turn into skateboards . . . . . Hundreds and hundreds of skateboards hanging from a skateboard tree . . . . . Notice the color and size of the skateboards . . . . . Now half of the skateboards turn into baseballs, and the other half become baseball bats . . . . .

Now the baseballs and baseball bats turn into stars and moons . . . . stars and moons hanging from the big green tree . . . shining . . . . . Let the stars and moons become forks and spoons . . . . . silver forks and spoons hanging from the branches . . . Now let all the forks and spoons turn into big yellow roses . . . . . Let the roses turn red . . . . . Let the red roses turn back into apples.

Now let's stand back and watch the red apples change colors. First they all turn yellow . . . then all of them are sky blue . . . . . Now let's make the apples in the top half of the tree turn white, and the bottom half can turn pink . . . . . Now turn the apples at the bottom violet, and the apples at the top, silver . . . . . Next, let's turn all the green leaves to silver and the apples to gold . . . . . Now let's turn the leaves to red and the apples to green . . . . . Now let's turn the leaves back to their usual green, but let the apples turn every color of the rainbow . . . .

Now let the apples stay all the different colors of the rainbow, but make them grow larger and larger until they begin to look more like balloons than apples . . . . . Balloons of every color . . . . . They are balloons, and as you watch, they begin to leave of the branches of the tree and slowly float upwards . . . . . All the balloons of every color are now floating gently up to the sky . . . . . You watch them as they grow smaller and smaller . . . . Look back at the apple tree, standing there very proud of all the images it was able to present to you . . . . And now please come back to this classroom. Feel the floor under your feet and the chair that is holding you up. Do not remove your blindfolds.

GROUNDING
Not yet, but in just a minute, I will ask you to take off your blindfolds and draw. Today I'd like you to draw the apple tree in one of its many changes. Choose one that you saw clearly or one that you particularly liked. If you have extra time, you can use the back of the paper to represent something else from this exercise. If you have any questions, please raise your hand, and I will come over to your desk. Do not talk, please. Ready, begin.

During the drawing, draw your picture and then circulate.

SHARING
As usual, ask for volunteers to tell about their pictures and to show them, if they wish. This exercise usually results in some lovely pictures that are shown with pride.

EVALUATION
Collect the papers, but do not evaluate them except to note the effort that was made.

THE NATURE JOURNEY

MATERIALS NEEDED
For Each Student
Unlined paper, crayons, and blindfold.

PREPARATION
- Remind students to watch their "movie screens."
- Distribute materials.
- Dim lights as a signal to put blindfolds on.

RELAXATION
Be sure your feet are flat on the floor.... Shake out your shoulders .... Now put your hands on your desktop and sit with your back straight and relaxed.... as if your head were a round ball resting gently on a column of golden building blocks... Let gravity and balance, not your muscles, do the work of holding your body upright .... See if you notice any tense places in your body today.... Let them relax as much as you can.... Remember that we are trying to become both relaxed and alert, calm and ready.

Start today by focusing your attention on your feet. Tense every muscle in your feet. Do not tense any other part of your body if you can help it.... Squeeze only the muscles in your feet, tighter and tighter.... tighter..... and tighter..... and then let all the tension go.... Take a deep breath all the way in..... and all the way out....

Now try to tense only the muscles in your legs and knees and thighs, not your feet... Do not tense any other muscles but those in your legs and knees and thighs.... tighter... tighter... tighter... now let all that go.... Take a deep breath all the way in... and all the way out......

Now your shoulders and arms and hands..... tighter... tighter... tighter... and then let go.... Take a deep breath, all the way in.... and all the way out....

Now, lastly, tense the head and neck and all the parts of your face. Your mouth, nose, forehead, cheeks, eyes, ears, everything, tense them all up tighter ... tighter... tighter... and tighter.... Now let it all go.... Now we will take just two more deep breaths, all the way in... and all the way out.... and all the way in.... and all the way out.....

VISUALIZATION

In your mind today, I want you to see a large mountain, the kind that looks like an enormous triangle. Very wide on the bottom, and pointed at the top..... Put snow on this mountain, just on the top..... Now turn the snow blue and the rest of the mountain pink..... Make the snow orange and the rest of the mountain red..... Make the snow green and the mountain white...... .Make the snow white and the mountain brown..... Now turn the mountain upside-down..... It is resting on its top..... Now make the mountain float up into the air and disappear.

Where the upside-down mountain was, you now see a large blue lake..... In the middle of the lake is a sailboat..... The sails have blue and yellow stripes ..... An elephant is sailing the boat..... The stripes on the sails turn black and white..... and the elephant becomes a giraffe..... Turn the giraffe into a kangaroo..... Make the sails red with a golden sun in the center..... Watch the kangaroo sail the boat as the wind comes up and blows the sailboat across the lake and out of sight.

Now where the sailboat had been, a motorboat appears..... It is racing around in a large circle, pulling a water-skier. You notice that the water-skier is actually a hippopotamus . . . skiing on all four feet with four water-skis . . . . . Turn the hippo into a camel . . . . . The camel is also on four skis . . . being pulled by the motorboat . . . . . Now the camel is going to try to water-ski on its front feet only, holding its back legs up in the air . . . . . Now he tries skiing on one foot . . . . . Turn the camel into a seal . . . . . The seal tries water-skiing by balancing on his nose with his tail up in the air . . . . . The seal is gray . . . . . Turn it yellow . . . . . turn it red . . . . . turn it blue . . . . . . have it balance a baby duck on its tail . . . . .

Now the boat and seal turn and race away, leaving the baby duck . . . . . As you watch, the baby gets bigger and older until it is a fully grown duck. The duck is white, with an orange bill . . . Now make this large duck orange . . . . . Make it pink and white . . . . . Make it blue and green . . . . . Turn it back to white with a yellow bill . . . . . Let it get smaller and smaller until it is just the right size for a duck . . . . .

Look up at the sky. It is a perfectly clear, blue sky . . . . . Keep it that same color blue. Now the stars come out . . . . . stars in the daytime . . . . . The moon comes up . . . . . The sky gets darker and the stars and moon get brighter . . . . . The sky is light blue again and the stars and moon disappear . . . . . A flock of geese flies overhead . . . . . And a hawk is circling . . . . . A jet flies by . . . . . A cloud comes along and drops light rain on the lake . . . . . The rain ripples the surface of the lake . . . . . The rain stops and the cloud is blown away . . . . . Now see a big rainbow in the sky above the lake . . . . . Now come back to the classroom . . . . . Feel your feet on the floor and the chair beneath you. Do not take your blindfolds off yet.

GROUNDING
Not yet, but in just a minute I will ask you to take off our blindfolds and draw anything you saw in your imagination. If you have time and would like to, draw more than one image. Use both sides of the paper, if you wish. If you have any questions, please raise your hand, and I will come to your desk. No talking please. Ready, take off your blindfolds and begin.

After you finish your picture, circulate around the room. You will be surprised to see how your students 'saw' some of your directions.

SHARING
Ask for a few volunteers as usual.

EVALUATION
Collect, but do not grade.

EXTENDED ACTIVITIES

Here are some ideas for developing further Journeys similiar to those provided in this chapter. They need not be a part of the basic program, but can provide further visualization experience now or later in the school year.

Use the following guidelines to help you plan your Journeys:
- Write out new scripts, drawing from the suggestions listed below.
- Experiment with programming or mind-mapping to help you plan your scripts.
- Try taping your script. Then, while listening to it, check your timing and correct mistakes.
- If you have a listening center and headphones, let students listen to your tapes individually.

LISTEN-AND-SEE JOURNEYS ABOUT SHAPES
Create colored shapes—triangles, rectangles, circles, squares. Start with one and change its color, then its shape. Later put one shape inside another, or beside another and experiment with their colors. Let them bounce, grow or shrink, or move around. Make a shape turn into something appropriate, like turning a triangle and a circle into an ice cream cone, or turning a square and a triangle into a house with a steep roof.

LISTEN-AND-SEE JOURNEYS ABOUT STUDENTS' HOUSES
Tell students to visualize a visit to their own homes, changing the color of the walls, the rugs, the furniture. Have them move the furniture from one room to another and see how it looks. Put the furniture on the ceiling, put pictures on the floor. Have the popcorn popper malfunction and fill the house with popcorn up to their knees. Have the whole class come over to eat it.

LISTEN-AND-SEE JOURNEYS ABOUT STUDENTS' OWN BACKYARDS

Direct the students into their own backyards. Change the size and shape. Change the weather. Change the color of the grass, trees, or flowers. Put in different kinds of fences, different trees, waterfalls, rocks. Now tell students to change their yards to their idea of the perfect yard. Put in equipment, a swimming pool, a tetherball, a soccer field, a pet elephant, anything they might want. Next have them bring in people to share their new yard. Image children, adults, and animals.

LISTEN-AND-SEE THE ZOO

Direct the students to picture going to the zoo. Turn the animals different colors. Have them stand on their hind legs, their front legs, or balance on one leg. Watch them eat. Give them better cages, adding trees, swimming pools, and other comforts.

LISTEN-AND-SEE A VEHICLE

Start with a car. Tell students to pick the model and color. Then change its color and size, have it grow wings and become an airplane. Let the airplane land in the water, lose its wings, and become an ocean liner. Have the ocean liner shrink and become a motor boat, and then a canoe. Let the canoe sprout wheels and become a wagon. Give it a cover, and it becomes a covered wagon. Change its colors. Have it travel over deserts and mountains, across rivers, through forests, and into a modern city. Let the wagon turn into a truck. End the Journey with the students' personal choices of the last vehicle.

4
Archetypes

RATIONALE

Webster's definition of *archetype:* "the original model, form, or pattern from which something is made or from which something is developed."

Because each of us comes equipped with a set of archetypes, we use those ready-made images as a first step in developing the skill of visualizing characters. For instance, we have a vivid notion of wicked witch-ness. When we read or hear of a character, we compare it with our idea or archetype. We immediately know whether we are confronting a wicked witch or not, regardless of the description of clothing and appearance given by the writer.

To fully appreciate a story, it is usually very important to be able to get a solid sense of the main characters, their strengths, weaknesses, needs, and desires. By beginning with archetypes whose characteristics are well known and widely agreed upon, students get practice in bringing storybook characters to life.

DESCRIPTION

Blindfolded, students will be asked to image a common archetype (wicked witch, kind mother, handsome prince). Students will then direct these archetypes to speak and take action.

PURPOSE

To begin to image characters and 'hear' speech. These activities will prepare students to build a set of prediction skills based on what they know of a character's personality.

SCHEDULING

Time needed for each lesson: 45-50 minutes
Number of lessons: Three
Extended activities: For optional development.

✤ Archetypes

ARCHETYPES ON PARADE

MATERIALS NEEDED
For Each Student
Unlined paper, crayons, pencils, and a blindfold.

For The Teacher
A chart with the names of the following archetypes written in large letters: Beautiful Princess, Wicked Witch, Kindly Old King, Wizard, Good Fairy, Big Bad Wolf, Handsome Prince, Wise Old Woman.

PREPARATION
- Tell your students that they are going to experience a new kind of Journey, one on which they will learn more about characterization.
- Talk to students about a magic wand. Tell them that visualization is in their own imagination, under their own control. Sometimes, when we are imagining, just as when we are dreaming, we create images that we do not like, and that we want to get rid of. In the imaging we are about to do in class, we are going to provide ourselves with a simple tool that will help in any situation. Each student will have a magic wand which cannot be lost or stolen. It is always there if you call on it. You may be using it in your Journey today, not to deal with any trouble, but to help you accomplish some things you want to do. In future Journeys, you can call on this magic wand at any time.
- Distribute the materials, and have students fold their paper into fourths and then open it again, providing a total of eight squares, front and back.
- Dim the lights as a signal to put on blindfolds.

RELAXATION
Please put your feet flat on the floor and begin to relax and center yourself.... Move your shoulders and arms and hands around as you like, and then put them on your desk tops.... Take a few deep breaths, all the way in, letting the oxygen travel all the way down into your lungs and stomach... and all the way out..... And again all the way in, this time letting the air go into your legs and all the way down to your feet and toes.... And all the way out....

We are going to begin today by going to a place where you love to be alone. . . . A place where you always feel safe and good. . . . . It could be outdoors . . . or indoors . . . It might be in your own house, or in someone else's. . . . . It might even be a place that you have read about or imagined. . . . Think of this place where you feel relaxed and safe and very good. . . . . And wherever it is, go there right now in your imagination. Feel yourself being there. . . . Notice the things you see there. . . . Look to the left. . . . . and to the right. . . . Look up and notice what you see. . . . and look down. . . . Now pay attention to the sounds in this place. . . . . . This is your own place. . . . and if you haven't thought of a place that fits my description of comfort and safety, then you can use your magic wand right now to create one. . . .

You can also use your magic wand to improve this place in any way you like. . . You can add improvements like furniture. . . . Or buildings. . . . . or more warmth or coolness. . . . Whatever you like and whatever you need. . . . . And now I will be quiet for a moment while you just enjoy being in this place of your own. . . .

Now, wherever you are, I would like you to notice that there is now a stage over to one side. . . . Notice its color and size. . . . The curtains are closed. . . . Very soon some characters are going to come out on this stage. . . . Let the lights in the room or in the sky begin to grow dim, so that you can easily see the stage, and you notice that the stage lights are starting to come on. . . . Get comfortable so that you can watch the show. . . . The curtains are about to part . . . .

VISUALIZATION

As the curtains pull back, you see a Beautiful Princess in the middle of the stage . . . . Notice the color she is wearing. . . . Does she wear anything on her head? . . . . Is she holding anything? . . . . Do you hear any sounds? . . . . Watch to see what she is doing. . . . .

Now the Beautiful Princess disappears, and in her place you see a Wicked Witch. . . . Notice what she is wearing. . . . Notice how she walks. . . . Is she carrying anything?. . . . Listen to any noises you hear. . . . . See what she is doing. . . .

♣   **Archetypes**

Now the Wicked Witch disappears, and in her place you see a Kindly Old King. . . . . Is he standing or sitting? . . . . . What is he wearing? . . . . . Notice the color . . . . . Take a look and see what he is doing . . . . .

The Kindly Old King disappears . . in his place you see a Wizard . . . . . Notice what the Wizard is wearing . . . . . what he might be holding . . . . . Notice his size . . . . . And see the color of his clothing . . . . . Does he have anything on his head? . . . . . Watch what the Wizard is doing . . . . .

Now the Wizard disappears, and in his place you see a Good Fairy . . . . . Is she carrying anything? . . . . . . What do you notice about her clothes? . . . . . What do you notice about her face? . . . . . What do you think she wants? . . . . . . Do you hear any sounds? . . . . . Now the Good Fairy disappears . . . . . and in her place you see the Big Bad Wolf . . . . . Notice how he walks . . . . . Watch what he is doing . . . . . . Do you hear any sounds? . . . . . What do you think he wants? . . . . . Does he look like a wolf you might see in a forest, or is he different from that? . . . .

And now the Big Bad Wolf disappears and in his place you see the Handsome Prince . . . . . Is he standing or sitting? What is he standing or sitting on? . . . . . Is he tall or short? . . . . . Is he dark or fair? . . . . . What is he wearing? . . . . . If he were looking for something, what do you think that might be? . . . . .

Now the Handsome Prince disappears, and instead you see a Wise Old Woman . . . . . What is this Wise Old Woman wearing? . . . . . What color is her hair? . . . . . Notice her face, her eyes . . . . .

Now the Wise Old Woman disappears, and the lights on the stage turn yellow . . . then orange . . . then red . . . then blue . . . and then they go out, and you come back here to this room, feeling the floor under your feet and the chair supporting you.

GROUNDING
Not yet, but in just a minute I will ask you to remove your blindfolds (or open your eyes). On your paper you have a total of eight squares: four on the front and four on the back. Your job is to describe a different character in each of the

squares. You may either draw the character, or write words or sentences to describe the character. Or, if you wish, you can draw a picture and then add words to further describe or explain the character.

Please label each picture with the name of the character. I will put up this chart to refresh your memory. Some of you may not have a chance to complete all eight squares. You may quickly fill all eight squares, or just concentrate on a few.

Remove your blindfolds now. Please raise your hand if you have any questions, and I will come to your desk.

As usual, circulate during this time, clarifying directions and encouraging students in their work. From this point, it is not so important that you always make a drawing with your students.

SHARING
Ask each student to show and/or read a description of one of the characters. It is fun, after one student has described an archetype, to ask how many others saw some of the same details and characteristics. Share the term *archetype* with your students and point out that we all have images for archetypes inside our heads. This visualization is not as personal as the memories were, so you can begin to call on students who have not previously shared.

EVALUATION
With this exercise, begin to give students more feedback about the effort you want them to put forth. You can begin to give evaluations with a check system. Give a plain check if the student has done about the expected amount of work, a plus mark if the student has done more work than expected, and a minus if the work is minimal. This evaluation is based solely on the effort the students make in translating their images into pictures and words. You might wish to postpone evaluating the rare student who still is not able to visualize clearly enough to create images. Consider making tapes for this student to listen to independently.

❖ Archetypes

ARCHETYPES' DILEMMA

MATERIALS NEEDED
For Each Student
Unlined paper, pencils, and blindfold.

For The Teacher
A chart, on the chalkboard or paper, with the names of archetypes: Poor Orphan Girl, Wicked Witch, Beautiful Princess, Wizard, Foolish Son, Good Mother, Big Bad Wolf, Good Fairy.

PREPARATION
- Tell students they will be working with the archetypes again, some the same and some new. Their job will be to get a feeling for the predictability of certain kinds of characters. You might discuss what we mean when we say someone acted "out of character."
- Distribute materials. Have students fold paper in fourths, open it out, and label each square with the name of an archetype copied from your list.
- Tell students that today they may use the blindfolds, or merely close their eyes and keep them closed when signaled. Give them the responsibility of choosing the way that helps them get the clearest and most consistent images.
- Dim lights as signal to put on blindfolds or shut eyes.

RELAXATION
First, put your feet flat on the floor and begin to relax and center yourself.... Move your shoulders and arms and hands as you wish to center yourself in gravity.... Remember that you want gravity to do the main job of holding you upright.... Now put your hands on your desk if they are not there already.... And take a deep breath, all the way in .... and all the way out.... Once more, all the way in .... And all the way out....

Now, return to the place that you created in your imagination yesterday... the place where you enjoy being alone... the place where you feel completely safe and comfortable... Feel yourself in that place.... Notice the sights you see..... and the sounds you hear..... and the things that you can feel here..... Take a moment to enjoy this place.... If you like to walk here... or run ... or climb... or swim... or sit... anything that you would like to do to explore or experience this place you can do now.... Now please return to the place where you saw the stage before and take a seat before it.... Again take notice of its size and color; it might be the same as yesterday or quite different.... Again the curtains are closed. . . . The lights in the sky or the room are growing dim, and the stage lights are being turned on . . . . Make yourself comfortable and get ready to see what the characters are going to do today . . . .

VISUALIZATION
Now look at the stage . . . . . The curtain is about to part . . . . . As it parts, you see a little lost kitten in the middle of the stage . . . . . Notice its color . . . . . Notice its size . . . . .

This is a "pretend" kitten; we are pretending it is here and pretending that it is lost so we can learn more about the characters we are about to see. We are going to find out what different characters would do if they were walking along and found this poor lost kitten.

The first character to come along is the Beautiful Princess. Watch and see what she does when she finds the lost kitten . . . . . Listen for anything that you might hear, and watch to see what she does . . . . (Wait twenty seconds) *. . Now bring that to a close and let the Beautiful Princess disappear.*

Use your magic wand to put the kitten back where it was before, alone and lost on the stage . . . . . here comes the Foolish Son . . . . . Notice what he is wearing and what he looks like . . . . . How can you tell he is the Foolish Son? . . . . . Now watch and listen to what he does with this little lost kitten . . . (Wait twenty seconds) *. . Now let that story end . . . . . The Foolish Son is gone now . . . . . use your magic wand to put the kitten back in the middle of the stage, alone and lost again . . . . .*

The next character who comes along and finds the little lost kitten is the Wizard . . . . . What will he do? Watch and listen . . (Wait twenty seconds) *. . Now bring that story to an end . . . . . Let the Wizard go . . . . . .and put the kitten back where it was before . . . . .*

Next you see a Poor Orphan Girl . . . . . Notice what she is wearing and how she seems to feel . . . . . Now watch and listen to find out what she will do when she sees the lost kitten . . (Wait twenty seconds) *. .And now that story ends . . . . . Let the Poor Orphan Girl disappear and put the kitten back on the stage alone.*

❖ **Archetypes**

In comes the Good Mother . . . . . Notice first what the Good Mother looks like . . . See her face . . . and what she is wearing . . . . . Now see what she will do with this little lost kitten . . (Wait twenty seconds) . . Now let that story end . . . . . and the Good Mother disappear . . . . . Put the kitten alone again on the stage . . . . .

Now along comes the Big Bad Wolf . . . . . See what happens as the Big Bad Wolf meets the little lost kitten . . (Wait twenty seconds) . . Now let that story end and let the Big Bad Wolf disappear . . . . . Use your magic wand to put the kitten back on stage again . . . . .

Now along comes the Wicked Witch . . . . . Watch and listen to find out what the Wicked Witch will do when she finds the little lost kitten . . (Wait twenty seconds) . . . Now let this story end and the Wicked Witch disappear . . . . . Put the little lost kitten back on the stage . . . . .

And here comes our last character, the Good Fairy . . . . . See what the Good Fairy will do when she finds the little lost kitten . . . (wait twenty seconds) . . . Now bring that story to an end. Let the Good Fairy disappear . . . . . Let the little lost kitten disappear . . . . . and come back to the classroom, feeling the floor under your feet and your chair supporting you.

GROUNDING

Please do not open your eyes yet, or take off the blindfolds. In just a minute, when you do open your eyes, I want you to write something on your papers. You have already made a square for each of the characters in today's Journey. Now I want you to write in each square what that character did with the little kitten.

If you saw the Beautiful Princess kiss the kitten and turn it into a Handsome Prince, then write that. If, on the other hand, she just stared at it and couldn't decide what to do, write that. Just describe what you saw. If you forget what one of the characters did, then just shut your eyes and imagine again, and then write that down. You can be brief. Write just enough to help you remember what each character did. For some of the characters, you could probably write a long story, but you just have a little square, so be brief.

If you have any questions, raise your hand, and I will come to your desk. No talking please; ready, begin.

Since the students are not accustomed to imaging without blindfolds, they may try to open their eyes as soon as the Journey is over. Discourage this, although it cannot be completely controlled. If they open their eyes and begin looking around, they may not be able to concentrate on your directions while still holding the images in their minds. Scan the room, and when you see eyes opening, go over and whisper or indicate that the eyes need to be closed. If a student cannot keep eyes closed, you might suggest a blindfold for the next Journey.

During the drawing period you can circulate and talk quietly to the workers. Your own drawing is optional.

SHARING
Ask students to share their favorite stories. This can be done as a whole class or with learning partners or in small groups. It is fun to ask how many students saw similar events for the same characters. This also helps them understand the concept of archetype and character consistency. They really enjoy hearing each other's ideas on the Journey.

EVALUATION
If you wish to grade the papers, use the check, plus, minus system, evaluating students on their efforts only.

❖ Archetypes

ARCHETYPES' WISHES

MATERIALS NEEDED
For Each Student
Lined paper, pencil, and blindfold.

PREPARATION:
- Distribute materials. Have students write the names of the following archetypes, leaving two lines blank after each name: Handsome Prince, Big Bad Wolf, Poor Orphan Girl, Kindly Old King, Wise Old Woman. Following the list of names and blank lines, write the words "I choose . . ."
- Ask students how it went for those without the blindfolds. Remind them to choose whichever option helps them to visualize. Suggest that any who had trouble keeping their eyes closed should go back to the blindfolds for a day or two. Be sure to give blindfolds to all students, even if they think they won't use them. They may change their minds part way through.
- Dim lights as a signal for blindfolds and closing eyes.

RELAXATION:
Please put your feet flat on the floor . . . . and move your shoulders and arms until your hands are ready to settle on your desktop . . . . . Now take a deep breath, getting your mind and body relaxed and alert, all the way in . . . oxygen flowing into your lungs and down all the way to your toes, and all the way out . . . stale air and stale thoughts leaving your body . . . . Again, all the way in . . . and all the way out . . . . . Now breathe normally, and center your body in space . . . lean just a little to the left and the right, back and forth, only a little each way, back and forth . . . until you find the center of gravity of your body . . . . Then lean a little forward and back, just a little bit each way, looking for the place where you feel perfectly balanced . . . .

And now that you are balanced, imagine once more a golden thread fastened to the top of your head, tugging gently upward so that it supports all of the weight of your head . . . . . Your head feels completely weightless, supported as it is by this golden thread . . . Notice the feeling of being centered in space and at the same time having your head held and balanced by this golden thread . . . . .

Notice now if there are any places in your body where you are holding tension today . . . . . . and allow golden light to travel down the golden thread . . . . and flow in through the top of your head . . . . Feel the golden light enter your body and travel to the spots where you are feeling the most tension . . . . The golden light warms and relaxes the tense places . . . . . Traveling down the golden thread, through the top of your head and spreading all through your body, but especially to warm and relax the tense places . . . .

Now I would like you to return again to the place where you like to be alone. Go to the place where you feel safe and comfortable. Look around again today, and see what things look like . . . . And now turn to the stage, and get seated, ready to view today's action . . . . Lights begin to dim, and the stage lights begin to glow . . . .

VISUALIZATION
As the curtain parts today, you see a hooded figure that you have not seen here before. This is the Wish Granter. The Wish Granter is in the mood to grant one wish today. Since there are many characters who visit this stage, the Wish Granter wants to learn the dearest wish of each of the characters. When all of the wishes are known, you will help the Wish Granter to choose the one wish that will come true.

The Wish Granter begins to call the characters, one by one. The first called is the Handsome Prince . . . There is a puff of smoke . . . notice the color . . . then, as the smoke clears, you see the Handsome Prince standing there, looking a little startled . . . He sees the Wish Granter and hears the words: I am in the mood to grant one wish today. Perhaps it will be your wish that I grant; perhaps it won't. Tell me, that I may decide wisely, what is your dearest wish, Handsome Prince?

The Handsome Prince thinks for a moment and then answers. You must listen to what he says . . . . . What is the Handsome Prince's dearest wish? . . . .

❖ **Archetypes**

Now the Prince disappears, and you hear the Wish Granter call the name of the Poor Orphan Girl . . In another puff of smoke, she appears . . . . . She is surprised to see the Wish Granter and to hear these words: I am in the mood to grant one wish today. Perhaps it will be your wish that I grant; perhaps it won't. Tell me, that I may decide wisely, what is your dearest wish, Orphan Girl? . . . The Girl thinks for a moment, and then answers . . . . Listen to her answer to learn the dearest wish of the Poor Orphan Girl.

The Orphan Girl disappears in the new puff of smoke as the Wish Granter calls the name of the Big Bad Wolf. . . Notice the color of the smoke . . . The Big Bad Wolf sees the Wish Granter and hears the words: I am in the mood to grant one wish today. Perhaps it will be your wish that I grant; perhaps it won't. Tell me, that I may decide wisely, what is your dearest wish, Big Bad Wolf?

The Big Bad Wolf thinks for a moment, and then answers . . . You must listen closely to his answer to learn the dearest wish of the Big Bad Wolf . . . .

The Big Bad Wolf vanishes when the Wish Granter calls the name of the Kindly Old King . . . . The Kindly Old King enters in his puff of smoke . . . He sees the Wish Granter and hears the words: I am in the mood to grant one wish today. Perhaps it will be your wish that I grant; perhaps it won't. Tell me, that I may decide wisely, what is your dearest wish, Kindly Old King?

The King thinks for a moment, and then answers . . . You must listen to what he says to discover his dearest wish . . . .

Now the Kindly Old King disappears as the wish granter calls the name of the Wise Old Woman . . . In a puff of smoke, the Wise Old Woman appears, and hears the words of the Wish Granter: I am in the mood to grant one wish today. Perhaps it will be your wish that I grant; perhaps it won't. Tell me, that I may decide wisely, what is your dearest wish, Wise Old Woman?

The Wise Woman thinks for a moment, and then answers . . . You must listen to her answer to learn the wish of this Wise Old Woman . . . . . .

Now the Wise Old Woman disappears, and the Wish Granter turns to you . . . He asks you which wish you think should be granted . . . Should it be the wish of the Handsome Prince . . . . . the Poor Orphan Girl . . . . . the Big Bad Wolf . . . . . the Kindly Old King . . . . . or the wish of the Wise Old Woman . . . . . Think for a moment, and then answer . . . .

Immediately, the Wish Granter grants the wish that you have chosen. You have exactly one minute to watch and see what will happen as a result of that wish . . . (Wait exactly one minute. The mind's eye does not observe time in the same way that we usually do. One minute can be enough time for a whole lifetime to pass. If you always give the students the same length of time, they will learn to fit all of their adventures into this time framework. If they have not finished their Journeys when you call time, they can continue to use their mind's eyes to finish up during the grounding period.)

Bring this Journey to a close, using your magic wand if you need to, and come back now to our classroom . . . . . Feel the floor under your feet, and the chair supporting you . . . . . Notice the sounds in the room and outside . . . . .

GROUNDING
Please do not open your eyes or remove your blindfolds quite yet. In just a minute, you will find your paper with the names of today's characters. After each name, please write the character's dearest wish. If you cannot remember what the wish was, just close you eyes and listen for it. When you have written what each character wished for, then write the wish that you chose to come true. Write that wish in the last space, where you have already written the words, "I choose . . ." If you have any questions, please raise your hand, and I will come to your desk. Without talking: ready, begin.

During the grounding, circulate and monitor your students' work.

SHARING
Ask volunteers to tell which characters they chose, and what happened to them. Ask who else heard exactly the same wish from the same archetype.

Or, you might want to mention the archetypes one by one, asking students for the wish they heard. You will find many similarities, and some interesting differences.

Archetypes

The wishes that break stereotypes, like the Big Bad Wolf who wants to be understood, are thought provoking and can lead to a good discussion about the differences between archetypes and stereotypes. Archetypes and character predictions are useful in literature, but stereotyping our real life friends and acquaintances can be very limiting to us both.

To follow-up this exercise you might ask your students to write out the story that happened when they saw the wish granted. When students write after they have done some clear and interesting imaging, they usually write eagerly, with a natural sense of plot and with a better style.

An interesting question to pose here is to ask how many saw the Wish Granter as a woman. There is no reference to gender in the script, and yet most of my students assume the Wish Granter is a male.

EVALUATION
Use the check, plus, and minus system for this visualization exercise. If you do the follow-up exercise mentioned in the SHARING section, you could grade it in the way you usually grade students' writing efforts.

EXTENDED ACTIVITIES

Here are some ideas for creating new Journeys with the archetypes. You may use the same relaxation exercises that I used in this section, ending up with the stage.

For maximum effectiveness, write your visualizations out in full script form, and practice with the tape recorder before working with your class.

ARCHETYPES' DWELLINGS
Name six archetypes to appear on the stage, one by one. Allow thirty seconds to watch each one of them walk down the path to the place where they live. Notice what the dwelling is made of, its shape, its size, its color. Go inside only if you would like to. Remind your students to take their magic wands.

Possible grounding activities:
Draw one of the dwellings on a piece of art paper. If students also saw the inside, draw the inside of the dwelling on the back of the paper. Label the paper with the name of the archetype who lives there. The dwelling might have a name. Students who finish quickly could do another.

ARCHETYPES' PICNICS
Name six archetypes, one by one. Allow time for students to visualize what each archetype would plan for a picnic. Visualize friends, food, equipment, vehicle, games, and location.

Possible grounding activities:
Students draw the picnic of one of the archetypes. Include the setting, the people, the food, the games, everything remembered. Students could list all of the elements of the picnic if they would rather write than draw.

ARCHETYPES' FEARS
Select six archetypes to call to the stage, one by one. Students imagine one thing that the archetype hopes will never happen. Allow students twenty seconds to see what that event is.

Possible grounding activities:
Students write each archetype's name, and below it write the one thing that he or she hopes will never happen.

ARCHETYPES' GOOSE
Pick six archetypes. One by one, watch to see what each will do when he finds the goose that lays the golden eggs. Give the students twenty seconds with each archetype to let the story unfold. Next, tell them to list each archetype and what he or she does with the goose that lays the golden eggs.

Then, write out the story of one of the archetypes and the magic goose.

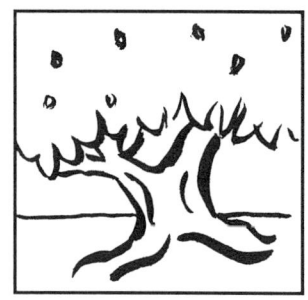

5
Characters and Settings

DESCRIPTION
Students will visualize while teacher reads descriptions of characters and settings. Movement and speech will also be directed.

PURPOSE
To teach students to create settings and characters from books and stories, so that these elements come to life in their own reading.

SCHEDULING
Time needed for each lesson: 30-45 minutes
Number of lessons: Five.

RATIONALE
The following exercises are designed to ensure that your students will experience literature filled with three-dimensional people and places. You will show your students how to bring to life the characters and settings found in stories they will read and hear. If students identify literary characters only by name and not by physical and emotional characteristics, much of the nuance of the plot is lost.

At first glance, this activity may not seem much different from plain oral reading. In many classrooms, teachers read stories to their students daily. The difference here is that before you read, you will tell your students what they are to picture while you read and what they will be expected to do with those pictures when you are finished. This anticipatory set helps your students to tune in on the kind of visualizing they should do on a regular basis in their own reading.

Your selection might also be from a book you intend to continue reading to your class as a part of your oral reading program. Or, you may select your passage from any other story with strong characterization or vivid descriptions of settings. Your librarian might offer further suggestions.

PREPARATIONS FOR EACH LESSON
- Tell students that you are going to read from a book while they close their eyes and visualize. Before you read, describe the Grounding Activity in detail, so that they will know what to create in their minds' eyes.
- Distribute the materials, and ask your students to put them inside their desks to eliminate distractions. Those who use blindfolds should keep them available.
- Dim the lights as a signal to close eyes or put on blindfolds.

RELAXATION FOR EACH LESSON
You may choose from among previous chapters, or just ask your students to center and take five deep breaths, talking them through each breath, all the way in . . . . . and all the way out . . . . . and so on.

VISUALIZATION AND GROUNDING ACTIVITIES
The following suggestions are included for the books listed above. Read a bit more slowly than usual, pausing between sentences to allow ample time for visualization.

Always tell your students what they will be asked to do after the reading. They can then concentrate on developing the images they will need for a successful experience.

BEN AND ME by Robert Lawson
In this book, the author describes the invention of the Franklin stove. Tell your students you are going to read the description and then ask them to draw a picture of their conception of the stove.

When the reading is finished, ask students to begin to draw imme-

MATERIALS NEEDED
For Each Student
Paper, pencil, crayons, and blindfold for optional use.

For The Teacher
A five-to-ten-minute passage from a favorite book for each lesson. You may choose readings from the following list of books which are included in the Grounding Activities section:
BEN AND ME
by Robert Lawson,
MRS. FRISBY AND THE RATS by Robert C. O'Brien,
WHERE THE RED FERN GROWS by Wilson Rawls,
STEWART LITTLE
by E.B. White,
THE BLACK PEARL
by Scott O'Dell,
ACROSS FIVE APRILS
by Irene Hunt, and
TIME AT THE TOP by Edward Ormondroyd.

❖ **Characters and Settings**

diately. If your class asks you to repeat your reading, that is acceptable, especially in a description as detailed as this one.

MRS. FRISBY AND THE RATS by Robert C. O'Brien
The description of the entrance to the intelligent rats' burrow provides an excellent passage to read to your class. Before you begin, let your students know that you will ask them to draw their conception of how that entrance looks from the outside.

After the reading, you might also ask them to list seven words that describe that entrance.

WHERE THE RED FERN GROWS by Wilson Rawls
The first pages of this book give a vivid description of an old stray hound who is being attacked by a pack of hunting dogs.

For the Grounding Activity, ask your students to write answers to questions you have created about the dog's appearance, personality, and other distinguishing features. Remember to prompt students to visualize, to go a step beyond the book's literal description.

STUART LITTLE by E. B. White
In the first chapter, Stuart descends into the drain on a string to rescue Mrs. Little's lost ring. Ask your students to describe the descent and the inside of the drain to a partner.

After reading this selection, you might also ask the partners to make a joint drawing.

THE BLACK PEARL by Scott O'Dell
When you finish the description of the Manta Diablo, have students work in pairs and describe the creature to each other, using gestures to show its size.

Suggest that one partner ask questions of the partner who is narrating.

ACROSS FIVE APRILS by Irene Hunt
Before you begin, ask your students to image in great detail the two charac-

ters you will read about. Tell them they are going to write a letter telling a friend that he or she is supposed to pick up the characters at the bus station. To help the friend identify the characters, the letter must contain detailed descriptions.

Read the description found in the beginning of the book of Ellen and her son Jethro.

TIME AT THE TOP by Edward Ormondroyd
Tell your students that they will be describing an unusual elevator to a friend. The description must be so clear that the friend cannot confuse it with any other elevator.

In the book there is a detailed description of the elevator that figures prominently in the plot. After you have read the selection, ask students to write their own description.

SHARING
This will vary with the Grounding Activity you select. Some Grounding Activities, such as describing to a partner, have the sharing built in.

GENERAL SUGGESTIONS FOR GROUNDING ACTIVITIES
When you select other books to read to your class, you might adapt some of the activities that follow or create others closely related to your story.
- Give students a list of ten questions about a character. Ask questions that require them to extrapolate or predict. Do not ask for specific details stated in the author's words.
- Ask students to list seven words that describe a character, physically and emotionally.
- Remember, the activities should always elicit more details as students visualize beyond literal interpretations.
- There are no right or wrong answers. Grounding Activities should allow for much diversity and creativity.

EVALUATION
I grade these by giving a check to those who do what is expected of them in terms of effort, a plus for extra effort, and a minus for very little effort.

6
Magic Journeys

DESCRIPTION
Students will be guided through an adventure in which they are the main characters. The teacher will develop the situation, then ask students to complete the Journey independently.

PURPOSE
To help students develop abilities to predict actions and provide solutions independently. This activity can have great impact on the quality of students' writing by giving them something meaningful to write about.

SCHEDULING
Time needed for each lesson: 45-50 minutes
Number of lessons: Three
Extended Activities: For optional development.

RATIONALE
In the set of scripts that follows, your class will be given time to watch and see what happens next. The students themselves are the central characters in a magic Journey. In this way they take a fully active part in how the story evolves and ends. They watch the drama unfold with all the richness and detail that their own imagination can bring to it.

They don't consciously think of what will happen next, because an amazing thing occurs when we open the doors to visualization. As they visualize situations and events, the images begin to act seemingly of their own volition.

Actually, they are still in control of what they image. They can consciously change or alter it, just as they can their daydreams. But they can also choose to allow the action to take on its own life.

It is important that children understand that they are in control of their own images and daydreams. If a monster or other unpleasant image appears in one of their fantasies, they have the resources they need to vanquish it. This is the reason that I stress that they always have access to a magic wand that can help them out any time they choose to use it.

Generally, however, it is very rewarding to let imaging begin to take on its own direction, and then watch and learn from what happens. They usually find resources and wisdom that they didn't know they had.

Once students are allowed and encouraged to take the time and effort to image a story ending in this way, putting it down on paper is really not very difficult. They already know what they want to retell, and they don't want to leave any exciting detail out. As your students practice watching action occur in their minds' eyes, their reading will be enriched. This kind of imaging activity also stimulates creative writing. Time and again I have heard well-known authors describe this process of allowing images to unfold in their minds' eyes. Many credit the richness of their writing largely to this process of imaging.

THE WISE TEACHER JOURNEY

PREPARATION
- Tell students to prepare to use the movie screen in their minds' eyes. You will read a story and stop short of the ending. It will be up to them to let the rest of the story happen in their mind movie. Assure them that if they relax, the ending will appear before them.
- Distribute materials.
- Dim lights as a signal to close eyes or put on blindfolds.

RELAXATION:
Now put your feet flat on the floor... And shake out your shoulders and your arms and hands.... Put them gently on your desk top... Remember that you want to get in a relaxed but alert state... You are going to search for the center of gravity of your bodies. I want you to sit up straight, as relaxed as you can allow your body to be..... Now sway your whole body, not just your head alone, but your whole body, slightly to the left... then to the right... just slightly, go back and forth, noticing at what point you pass right through your center of gravity... Concentrate on that center, and keep slowly swaying.

MATERIALS NEEDED
For Each Student
Unlined paper, crayons, and blindfold.

. . . . a little less each time . . . . . until you come to rest right in your exact center of gravity. Here your body has to do very little work to keep upright, because you are centered in space.

Now we will do the same thing, this time moving forward and back. Sway slightly forward . . . . . and slightly back . . . . . then forward . . . . . and back . . . . . looking for the spot where you pass through your center of gravity . . . . As you find it, make your movements smaller and smaller until you stop exactly in your own center . . . . .

Notice how easy it is to be perfectly upright when you have found this center of gravity. You can be completely relaxed while still staying completely alert and ready for anything that happens. This kind of centering of the body is what judo and karate experts use to be fully alert. When we tense our bodies to face difficulty, we only slow them down. But when the body is in this state of calm alertness, it is ready for quick movement.

Be aware again of your own center . . . . . Shift slightly back and forth and return to the center once more . . . . . Shift a little to the left . . . and right . . . and then return to center . . . . .

Now take five deep breaths. (Time these to your own slow and deep breathing.) Breathe all the way in . . . . and all the way out . . . . (Repeat for a total of five.)

VISUALIZATION

On our Journey today you are walking along a dirt path in a broad valley. It is a lovely day, sunny and warm . . . . . You hear birds as they fly past you . . . . . Not far away you can hear the gurgling sounds of a mountain stream . . . You stop to listen . . . .

Looking all around, you see tall mountains everywhere . . . . . One of them looks more interesting than all the rest . . . . . You notice a wide path that will take you to the top of this mountain. You make up your mind to follow it all the way up. You check to make sure that you have your magic wand with you, and off you go . . . . .

At first the path is flat and easy to travel. You lean over to smell some blue and purple wildflowers . . . . . They tickle your nose . . . . . You are beginning to get quite warm as you walk along. The sun is shining on your back and on the top of your head . . . . . You move on more quickly to catch the slight breeze that is swaying the tall grasses . . . . . You are surrounded by the sweet grassy smells . . . . . . A doe suddenly breaks out from behind the grass and runs across the path a short way in front of you . . . and just as she disappears, a tiny fawn, just a few days old, runs across the path so close you can almost touch it . . . . .

You hurry along the path . . . . . You feel your legs moving beneath you and you hear your feet thudding on the soft dirt . . You are on your way to the top of this mountain to visit the wisest person in the world. You have heard that this wise person who lives at the top will answer questions and help anyone who wants to improve.

As you walk, you think of something that you would like to know how to do better . . . . . Maybe it is something in sports . . . . . maybe it is something in school . . . . . maybe it is a problem to solve . . . . . or with your friends . . . . . Whatever it is, you know that the wise person will be able to help you with it . . . so you hurry on . . . . .

The path begins to get steep. Then steeper and steeper . . . Notice what you see along the way up . . . .

Now you are nearing the top . . . . . If you are not at the top yet, use your magic wand to get yourself there . . . .

It is sunny up here, too, and you feel the warmth of the sun all over you . . . . . You have climbed the tall mountain and you feel exhilarated . . . . . You breathe in the fresh mountain air . . . . . Now you look around and notice the building where the wise person lives . . . . . You know that you will be welcome. You go in quietly.

In a large room, you see the wise person. This wise person looks like someone you know . . . or someone you have read about or seen in books . . . . . You notice that there is a resemblance to yourself as well.

❖ **Magic Journeys**

You have exactly one minute now to have a conversation with this wise person. Time to ask anything you want about as many things as you want. Listen carefully for the answers. You might have to repeat the question before you get your answer, but if you listen, it will come. Ready, begin. (Wait exactly one minute.)

Now, bring your conversation to a close. Remember that this is your very own wise person. And if there are more things you would like to talk about, you can always return to this mountain top and continue your discussion.

As you begin to say thank you and good-bye, the wise one brings out a golden box. It is shining with its own golden light . . . . . The wise person tells you that inside this box is a gift for you to take home. This gift will help you remember this Journey and what you learned from the wise person. You open the box to see what is inside . . . .

Now it is time to walk back down the mountain. Don't forget to bring your gift. Use your magic wand to help you carry the box if it too heavy . . . . Down and down you climb . . . . . passing again everything that you saw on your way up . . . . . . Then you reach the valley. If you are not there yet, use your magic wand to bring yourself there . . . . Walk back to the place where you to listened to the brook . . . . . Then back to this classroom . . . . . You feel the floor beneath your feet and the chair supporting you . . . . . Do not open your eyes or remove the blindfolds quite yet, but stretch and move a little if you like . . . . . .

GROUNDING
Not yet, but in a minute, I will ask you to take off your blindfold or open your eyes and draw. On one side of your paper, draw the gift that your wise person gave you to help you remember your Journey. On the back of the paper, show any other part of the Journey that you would especially like to remember. If you have any questions, please raise your hand, and I will come to your desk. Use your energy for the drawing. Ready, open your eyes and draw the gift on one side of the paper and any other scene on the back.

SHARING
Because of the personal nature of this journey, you may not want to have whole-class sharing. It is important that students relate their questions and answers or describe their gifts only if they wish to do so. Now is the time to

go around and assess this, getting a feeling for whether your students are eager or reluctant to tell others about their experiences. Depending on the grade level and the trust level of your class, you may wish to delete whole-class sharing entirely. If they wish to tell you about their experiences it is a good idea for you to draw and share with your students.

EVALUATION
As in the last few chapters, these papers can be evaluated on the basis of effort, with checks, pluses, and minuses.

A MAGIC FOOD JOURNEY

PREPARATION
- Tell students that again they will be creating a mind movie, and to relax and let the story flow.
- Distribute materials.
- Tell your students that they will be recording their Journeys as a cartoon writer does, showing what happens next in each box. Advise them to keep the drawing simple, or it will take far too long to record all their adventures. Tell them that they are welcome to use their pencils to add words to each box, if they like.
- Dim lights as a signal to put on blindfolds or close eyes.

MATERIALS NEEDED
For Each Student
Crayons, pencils, and unlined paper that has been divided into eight to ten boxes for a cartoon strip, and blindfold.

RELAXATION
Be sure that your feet are not crossed and are firmly set on the floor. Shake out your shoulders and arms and hands, and then put them gently on your desk top. Remember, you are relaxing your body, but you are not trying to fall asleep. You want to be relaxed and also fully alert . . . . Take five deep breaths. (Time these to your own slow and deep breathing.) *All the way in . . . . . and all the way out . . . . .* (Repeat for a total of five times.)

Now imagine that your body is made mostly of air and space. Imagine that you are so full of space that you are getting lighter and lighter. Your head almost floats upward instead of nodding down. You notice that your whole body is pressing less and less on the chair where you are sitting. You are growing so light that suddenly you notice that you are really beginning to float upward. You float like a balloon, up toward the ceiling . . . . . You realize that you can gently bounce all around the room, like the astronauts inside their space capsules. Motion is slow, but you can bounce anywhere . . . . You bounce off a wall . . . . off the ceiling . . . .off the floor . . . off the bookcase . . . Since you are mostly made of air, you don't disturb anything, but the papers do flutter as you pass by . . . .

Gently now, you will lower your spacious body slowly, slowly, down to your chair. Feel the floor beneath your feet again, and the chair underneath your body. Let your body rest comfortably, while you get ready to go on a Magic Journey.

Remember that you always have your magic wand to help you with any difficulty. Use it as you need to.

VISUALIZATION

Today you are walking down a path in a meadow on a fine spring day. You can feel the sun shining on your back and shoulders as you walk briskly along. Underfoot you feel the rough dirt path, and now and then you kick at a stone that is in your way . . . . . You feel the wind blowing lightly on your face and arms . . . . . and hear it blowing through the trees at the meadow's edge . . . . . It is a cool breeze, but your clothes keep you warm.

You are aware of the smell of pine trees and wildflowers . . . You look around to see the flowers all over the meadow . . . in colored patches. Orange flowers over there . . . . . and some yellow ones under the trees . . . . . Some blue . . . . . and there you see a little patch of tall red flowers . . . . .

Coming from the trees up ahead you hear a flurry of bird songs. You listen . . . . and try to see the birds as you pass the clump of trees . . . . . Just on the other side of the trees, you spy a palace.

It is a pleasant-looking palace, and your nose tells you that there is something very special about it. The most delicious combination of smells you can imagine is floating from it. Roast beef . . . . . pumpkin pie . . . . . chocolate cake . . . . . fresh bread . . . . . French fries . . . . . and many, many more wonderful smells . . . . . telling you that inside this palace must be every kind of delicious food that you have ever eaten.

As you walk toward the palace, you are wondering who owns this wonderful place, and whether they might invite you in. You have been walking a long time, and you are really quite hungry. As you get nearer, you notice a huge sign on the front door . . . . . It has your name on it . . . . and the words, "Welcome. Come in and help yourself to anything you want." You realize that this palace is here for no other reason than for you to enjoy. It is your imagination, your palace, and everything in it is yours. You open the door and go in.

Your nose was exactly right. Inside the palace you see and smell huge quantities of all your favorite foods. A never-ending supply of everything that you love to eat, and nothing you don't like. There is a room with nothing but chocolate. Great big swimming pools full of chocolate syrup, shelves stacked with chocolate bars, bins filled with chocolate chips. In another room are baked goods: doughnuts big enough to make into tire swings, bread sticks the size of stilts, and cookies as big as tables. In each room is another of your favorite kind of food. As you wander from room to room, you realize that it is all yours.

Now, I am going to give you exactly one minute of time. Do whatever you want to do in this palace of food. You can play in it, eat in it, swim in it, whatever you want to do. Ready, now. (Wait exactly one minute.)

Now, begin to bring this Journey to a close . . . . . Remember that you created this palace in your own mind, and whenever you want to go back, you can.

Use your magic wand if you need to clean yourself up and restore things to normal. Then walk out the door, back down the path . . . . . The sun is still shining, and the breeze is still blowing in your face . . . . . You can hear the birds singing as you walk back down the dirt path to where you started . . . . . Leave the smell of wildflowers and pine trees behind . . . . . and come back to this room . . . . . feeling the chair and the floor beneath you, supporting you . . .

♣ **Magic Journeys**

GROUNDING
Please keep your eyes shut until I give you the signal to draw something of what you experienced. You may draw the events in each square, as they happened to you. Put a different picture in each square.

Use a pencil or pen only when you wish to add words to your representation.

If you have any questions, please raise your hand, and I will come to your desk.

You can draw and circulate while your students are working.

SHARING
This is a good one to do the sharing in small groups.

EVALUATION
Grade effort only with checks, pluses, and minuses.

JOURNEY BEHIND A WATERFALL

MATERIALS NEEDED
For Each Student
Crayons, pencil, art paper, and blindfold.

PREPARATION
- Tell students that again they will be creating a mind movie, and to relax and let the story flow from where you leave off.
- Distribute materials. Explain to the students that they will be drawing a picture to record something from the Journey.
- Dim lights as a signal to put on blindfolds or close eyes.

RELAXATION
Be sure that your feet are uncrossed and are firmly set on the floor. Shake out your shoulders and arms and hands, and then put your hands gently on your desk top. Remember, you are relaxing your body, but you are also going to be fully alert . . . . Let's take five deep breaths. (Time these to your own slow and deep breathing.) *All the way in . . . . . . and all the way out . . . . .* (Repeat for a total of five times.)

As you take the next slow, deep breath, see the oxygen fill every corner of your lungs, cleaning and energizing as your lungs fill. And as you breathe out the old air, feel the tingling aliveness of your two clean, freshened lungs. . . . . . With the next breath, see the oxygen breathed all the way down into your stomach, cleaning and soothing as it goes . . . . . And as you breathe out, feel the relaxed and calm sensation inside and around the area of your stomach . . . . . Let the next breath travel down past your stomach, all the way into your upper legs, cleaning and soothing all the tension and tiredness from your muscles. . . . . And as you breathe slowly out, notice the feeling of aliveness and of relaxation in your upper legs. . . . . .Now let the next breath take fresh, soothing air down to your lower legs and calves, cleaning and relaxing all of the muscles in your lower legs . . . . . and as you breathe out, concentrate on the sensations of the relaxed and soothed muscles in your legs and calf muscles. Now let the next breath carry the oxygen all the way down to your ankles, and feet and toes. Feel each toe being cleaned and relaxed by the flow of oxygen. . . . . And as you slowly breathe out, feel how clean and calm and alive your toes and feet and ankles and legs are feeling. . . .

This time, let your breath enter your lungs and travel into your arms. Let the oxygen smooth out all of the tension in your muscles, and leave them feeling relaxed and energized . . . . . As you breathe out, notice the calm sensation in both of your arms . . . . . And now let your next breath travel all the way down your arms and into your wrists and hands and fingers, cleansing and relaxing all of the muscles . . . . As you slowly breathe the air out, pay attention to the gentle, relaxed feelings in your fingers and hands and wrists and arms . . . . . Now let the next breath enter your lungs and travel up to your head and your brain, cleansing and relaxing and refreshing your ears and eyes and nose and mouth, and bringing nourishment to your brain. . . . . And as you slowly breathe out, notice how refreshed, calm and alert your head is feeling. . . . . . . And now with your body calm and alert from the oxygen you have provided, you are ready to begin today's Journey.

VISUALIZATION
Today you find yourself by the edge of a lovely mountain stream. You are sitting on a large, gray, granite rock. Reach out with your hand and feel the texture of the rock beneath you. Notice how warm or cool it is under your fingers. Listen to the sound of this mountain stream as it passes by the place

where you are sitting. Dip your hands into the water and help yourself to a drink of this cool, clean, clear water. . . . . .Listen for other sounds besides that of the water. . .Are there birds singing in the trees?. . . . . .Is the wind rustling the branches of the trees?. . . . . .

You have been sitting on this rock for a while now, and you are ready to do a little exploring. You wonder what might be up ahead along the stream, so you stand and begin to follow this lovely stream to find out where it comes from. At first, it is easy going along the bank. There is dirt and grass, and you can easily walk alongside the water, listening to its babbling, almost as if it were singing a song just for you.

But soon the path grows a bit steeper, and there are more rocks in the water, and alongside the stream as well. You must begin to pick your way from one rock to another. Remember that your magic wand is always available when you need assistance, but you are enjoying the challenge of stepping from rock to rock. The sun is warm on the rocks and on your back as you begin to climb more steeply.

Soon you notice that the sound of the water from the stream is growing louder. . . . . . . .It is so loud that you can no longer hear the sound of the breeze in the branches, or even of the birds singing from the trees. And as you walk on it grows louder still. . . . . . .

While climbing up the rocks you lose sight of the stream for a minute, and when you reach the top of a particularly large rock you see the reason for the noise that the water is making. There before you is a waterfall. It is taller than the trees, and at least as wide as the walls in your own bedroom. The water in the fall is rushing down over the stone cliff, hitting so hard at the bottom that a cloud of white mist is thrown up. Below the mist, under the waterfall, you can make out a large, deep, green pool where the water from the fall rests before joining the stream in its journey down the mountainside. You stand for a moment, your eyes drinking in the sight of this lovely fall, your skin feeling the cool air and the droplets of moisture sprayed out by the cascading water. . . . . .You hear the roaring song of the waterfall. . . . . .

Then, feeling adventurous, you decide to see how close you can get to the falling water. You continue to climb the rocks along the side of the stream. They soon bring you to the edge of the pool . . . . You notice little water birds sitting on rocks by the water's edge and then suddenly diving into the water to catch their dinner . . . . You look at the colors in this deep, calm pool at the base of the fall, and you feel the mist on your cheeks and arms . . . .

Now you notice that there is a little stone path winding around the edge of this pool, leading you right up to the edge of the waterfall itself. You follow the stones through the mist. The path leads closer and closer to the fall, and then it winds around to the side and you see that it will take you behind the falling water. The noise from the water is very loud, but the path looks quite safe. You decide to follow the little stone path, and you go behind the waterfall. The roar of the water drives away all other sounds. You try to look through the rushing water, but you can only catch glimpses of the deep green pool and the stream beyond . . . . .

Something catches your attention and you turn around to look at the stone wall behind you, behind the waterfall. In the cool dimness of this little corridor between the waterfall and the wall of stone it is hard to see clearly, but you vaguely discern a door in the stone wall . . . . .

You have exactly one minute of time, which will be all the time you need, to open that door and to see what awaits you behind the door, behind the waterfall. Ready, begin. (Wait one minute.)

Now finish up your adventure. Use your magic wand if you wish, to complete or restore things to normal. Come back through the door in the stone wall . . . . .walk out the corridor between the wall and the waterfall . . . . . walk back by to the deep green pool . . . . .and back down the rocks. . . . . .and along the grassy path by the gentle mountain stream to the large rock where you sat before you begin your Journey . . . . . And now come back to this room, feeling yourself sitting in your chair with your feet firmly on the floor. Take a deep breath and slowly let it out.

GROUNDING
Please keep your eyes closed until I give you the signal to draw something of what you experienced. You may pick one thing that happened to you behind the

door and represent it on your paper. If you wish to add words, you can use your pencil for that. If you finish quickly, you can use the back of your paper to draw the waterfall.

If you have any questions, please raise your hand, and I will come to your desk. Ready, begin.

You can draw and circulate while the students are working.

SHARING
Students can tell of their adventures, sharing their pictures too, if they wish. After each brief story, ask if others saw similar sights, or had similar experiences.

EVALUATION
Grade efforts only with a check, plus, or minus.

EXTENDED ACTIVITIES

Be sure to write out your script and test it before using it with your class. Mind-mapping and patterning will help you with ideas and details. Or, visualize, write, visualize and then write. These scripts can also be used later in the year as an optional activity for either reading or writing. I think you will find that the quality of writing will be exceptional.

A MAGIC JOURNEY INTO A CLOUD
You are now so light that you can go right through the ceiling.

Look down on the school and the school year and on your friends' homes. See cars, streets, shopping centers. Include the senses in your Journey:
    HEARING: cars, people's voices from far-away, planes, birds.
    TOUCH: air, wind, clouds' mist, coolness.
    SMELL: fresh air, smoke from chimneys, exhaust from cars.

Look up and see a light, fluffy cloud. Go into it and have a one minute adventure inside the world of the cloud.

Now come back down to the school.

A MAGIC JOURNEY INTO THE HOUSE OF WISHES

Travel through a magic forest until you see an elf prince with his foot caught under a fallen tree. You use all your strength and stay in touch with your own center of gravity to move the tree and free him. As a last resort, you could use your magic wand.

He is so grateful that he gives you a magic key that will fit the lock in the door of the House of Wishes. You continue in the forest with him until you reach the House of Wishes. Include the senses in your Journey:
- HEARING: elf prince crying, wind blowing, tree creaking as you move it.
- TASTE: sweat as you work to move the tree.
- SMELL: forest dampness, the musty dirt around the tree as you move it.
- TOUCH: the tree, lever, the magic key, the door of the House of Wishes.

When you are at the door of the House of Wishes, the elf prince bids you farewell and good luck. You enter the House of Wishes and there you will have exactly one minute to make any wishes you would like. They will all come true. Watch and see how they turn out. Remember that your magic wand is always by your side in case you need it.

Now, leave the house, and return through the forest to your classroom.

A MAGIC JOURNEY TO BUILD A SPECIAL PLACE

It is your birthday. As a surprise, an unknown rich and kindly relative appears. For your birthday present this relative gives you an endless supply of building materials. Bricks, glass, wood, concrete, metal, and even gold, silver, and bronze, marble, and all kinds of beautiful stones. You can build any kind of structure you wish. You could build something for yourself, for your family, for the town, or even the whole nation. Include the senses in your Journey:
- HEARING: people sing "Happy Birthday," trucks and vans bring building supplies.
- TASTE: the birthday cake and ice cream.
- SMELL: the candles as you blow them out.
- TOUCH: all of the building materials.

From your centering exercise, you have grown very strong. Also you can use your magic wand as you build. You have one minute to see what you build, and what happens next. Now, you can dismantle the structure, or leave it there to return to some other time. Come back to the classroom.

A MAGIC JOURNEY THROUGH A LOOKING GLASS

Go to an old two-story house that an elderly aunt owns. While your parents are talking to her, you wander up the stairs to the attic. It is dusty and full of antiques. You trip, and a very old sheet falls on the floor. You see that it fell off of an ornate, full-length mirror. As you look, the mirror grows misty. You put out your hand, and it goes right through the glass. Include the senses in the Journey:

  HEARING: stairs creaking, dishes rattling from the tea that the adults are
    drinking downstairs.
  TASTE: some cookies and tea before you go upstairs.
  SMELL: dust, old perfume from a chest in the attic
  TOUCH: spider webs, a bannister, dust.

You examine your hand as you pull it back from the mirror and it looks fine. You decide to step through. You have one minute to see what will happen to you on the other side of the mirror.

Then step back through, go down the stairs to where the adults are still talking, never noticing your absence. Now come back to the classroom.

A good Grounding Activity: Have your students draw the mirror on one side of their paper as big as they can; then turn the paper over and hold it up against a window. Then trace the outline of the mirror onto the back of the paper and draw a picture of their adventure, on the back of the mirror.

A MAGIC JOURNEY TO THE BOTTOM OF THE SEA

You are out in a calm lagoon by a tropical island. A dolphin swims by and begins to talk to you. When she finds out that you are friendly, she asks for your help. Her son was nearly caught by a fisherman, and the hook is still in his mouth. It is very painful. Will you help? You use your magic wand to get the hook out easily. To thank you, the dolphin mother gives you the gift of being able to breathe under water. She invites you to jump off the boat

into the warm water of the lagoon and explore the world under the sea. Include the senses in your Journey:
    HEARING: ripples, waves, splashing fish, oars of your boat.
    TASTE: the salty spray on your lips.
    SMELL: salty air, sea spray.
    TOUCH: the hook, the dolphin's skin, the boat oars, the warm water.

You decide to go with her. You will have one minute to see what happens under the ocean. Then climb back into your boat and return to the shore. Then, you return to class.

Grounding Activity: Have students color their pictures with dark crayons. Then, put a light blue watercolor wash over the drawing to give it an underwater feeling.

A MAGIC JOURNEY INTO PARENTHOOD
It has been a bad day at home. Your parents have been upset with you all day. You couldn't seem to do anything right. You go to bed wishing that you didn't have to be a kid any more. Include the senses in your Journey:
    HEARING: your parents scolding you, the tock of the clock as you drift off
      to sleep.
    TASTE: dinner, glass of milk.
    SMELL: cooking, the garbage as you empty it.
    TOUCH: sheets and blankets, your pet.

When you wake up, you find that you are a parent, and your parent is now you. You have one minute to see how the day will go. Then you wake up and realize it was all a dream, and you come back to the classroom.

Grounding Activity: Ask your students to:
List two things they liked about being a parent.
List two things they didn't like about being a parent.
List two reasons why they prefer being a child.
List two things they don't like about being a child.

7
Create a Myth

DESCRIPTION
Students will be guided through a universal myth, up to the point of climax. They will then be given time to visualize a resolution and finish the myth.

PURPOSE
To extend work begun in Chapter Six to develop a sense of plot, working through conflict and resolution. Myths are used because the story line is so powerful that it draws the student to a clear and meaningful ending.

SCHEDULING
Time needed for each lesson: 60-70 minutes. Number of lessons: Three.

RATIONALE
The many valuable activities in this chapter help students gain a sense of plot resolution.

My students have greatly enjoyed these activities, and I have found that the depth and sensitivity of their writing during the grounding activities make this one of the top writing assignments of the school year.

According to Joseph Campbell in *Hero with a Thousand Faces,* a myth is a great deal more than just a story. He writes: ". . . the symbols of mythology are not manufactured; they cannot be ordered, invented, or permanently suppressed. They are spontaneous productions of the psyche, and each bears within it, undamaged, the germ power of its source."

When guided to deal with these symbols and the universal questions raised by the characters and heroes in the myths, the students are elevated to hero status themselves, and usually resolve the myth in such a way as to add to their own personal strength and true humanity.

Create a Myth ✤

BEAUTY AND THE BEAST

PREPARATION
- Tell your students to get their mind movie screens ready, as they are about to provide the end of a story. Remind them to relax.
- Distribute materials. Tell students that after you read part of a story, they will then see an end in their minds' eyes. Then, they will write down what they saw. They can illustrate the story as well, if they have time.
- Dim lights as a signal to put on blindfolds or close eyes.

MATERIALS NEEDED
For The Student
Lined paper and pencil for writing; unlined paper and crayons for drawing, blindfold.

RELAXATION
Please put your feet flat on the floor . . . Shake out your shoulders . . . shake your arms and hands . . . now put them gently on your desk top . . . Balance your spine so that gravity is doing the work of holding your body upright . . . . Sway back and forth a little until you find that center of gravity . . . . Let your body be relaxed and alert . . . . . Now take a slow deep breath, all the way in . . . . . and all the way out . . . . . . Now imagine that you are dressed in shorts and a light top, and you are standing in warm sand on a tropical island . . . . . You can feel the warm sand on the bottom of your bare feet and between your toes . . . . you wiggle your toes in the sand . . . . . The air around you is warm and heavy . . . . . there is no breeze at all . . . . Suddenly you hear the sound of big raindrops splattering on the leaves of the nearby trees, hitting your hair . . . . . your shoulders . . . your nose . . . . You know that there is no reason to run for cover, because the rain that comes every afternoon is always warm and pleasant, and no one cares if you get wet today . . . . So you stand there with your feet in the sand, ready to enjoy this tropical shower . . . . . As the raindrops come more quickly, you can hear them falling on the leaves of the trees . . . . . faster and faster . . . . and you feel each individual drop as it gently falls on your head . . . . and your

103

♣ **Create a Myth**

arms . . . . You turn your face up to the sky and the drops fall on your cheeks and chin and forehead, and on your closed eyelids . . . .

Now you turn your face back down, because the rain is heavier, still warm and gentle, but coming down in greater and greater amounts. So many raindrops are falling that the water begins to run off of you in little streams. Water streams off of your head, off your shoulders . . . . and down your back . . . . . You stand there, listening to the rain in the trees . . . . smelling the rain hitting the dry sand . . . . enjoying this shower of warm rain . . . . .

Now the rain slows . . . . . You can feel the individual droplets again . . . . and it stops . . . . . Notice the silence . . . . . then the birds begin to sing . . . . and the sun comes out to dry the water from the trees and the sand and you . . . . . Now you leave this warm island and return to our classroom, ready for today's Journey.

VISUALIZATION

On your Journey today, you are going to a tiny village in a kingdom of long ago and far away. Three equally beautiful sisters and their aging father live there. He is entirely kind and loving to everyone.

In this family, as in all good families, each member is quite unique.

The oldest sister loves knowledge. She is smart, witty, and well read. Everyone in the town comes to her when they have a problem. She either knows the answer or knows just what book to find it in.

The middle sister loves her home. She loves to keep house, sew a fine seam, and fill the house with the smells of good food and flowers from her father's garden. All the women in the village consult her if they need a pattern for a new dress or if they want to learn a new recipe to please their husbands and children.

The youngest daughter loves life itself. And in this family of beautiful girls, she is the most beautiful and loving of all. She loves her sisters and her home; she loves the village and the people in it. She loves her father's rose garden, and most of all she loves her father. She spends long hours helping her father in his garden, as he is getting older and cannot keep it so wonderfully without her tender care.

As much as the father loves his daughters, he loves his garden even more. And as much as he loves his garden, he loves his roses most of all. He has traveled the country over to find every kind of rose that graces the kingdom, and now his garden is the finest in all the land.

One day the oldest sister returns from a visit to a neighboring village and brings back a tale. She has heard of a wonderful rose that is said to be pure black. A black rose! The father is beside himself. He must have it. He will go to search for it and bring it back to his garden.

The sisters beg him not to go, but he is determined. So the middle sister gives him food for his journey, and the oldest sister gives him her best maps so he will not lose his way, and the youngest gives him hugs and kisses and a blessing for a safe journey . . . . .

Days pass, and he does not return. The three daughters are concerned and decide that someone should go after him. The oldest cannot go, because she is needed in the village to help solve problems and answer questions. The middle sister cannot go, for her home would get dusty and the flowers would wilt. So it is up to the youngest.

She takes the gifts of food from her middle sister and a map from her oldest sister, and off she goes to search for their dear father.

She goes over bridges . . . . . and through towns . . . . . down roads of dirt and roads of cobblestones . . . . . and finally she comes to a castle . . . . .

It is surrounded by a thorny hedge which towers above her head . . . . . She circles the hedge seeking an opening . . . . . At last she sees a tiny space and she squeezes through . . . . . In the courtyard is a garden even more beautiful than her father's.

Flowers and exotic plants laid out in dazzling arrays surround her . . . . . Charming paths set with colored stones wind through banks of deliciously scented blossoms . . . . . And at the center of this incredibly beautiful garden, in the place of honor, she sees the black rose, and she knows that her father must have come here.

♣ **Create a Myth**

Now she hears a man's voice from inside the castle. Strangely, she is not frightened. The voice is kind, almost apologetic. He tells her that her father broke into the garden and tried to steal the black rose. The castle servants captured him and locked him in the dungeon.

Sounding very sad, the voice tells her that he does not want to make her father suffer, but that his castle is a very lonely place and needs a girl's touch. Her father will be forgiven and released to return home only if she will promise to take his place and live at the castle. She will be treated well, given the finest food and clothes. Servants will wait on her, and her bed will be made of gold. But she will never be allowed to see the man behind the voice or to leave the castle.

She is frightened, but she loves her father so much that she cannot refuse the offer of his release. She agrees.

Her father comes out of the castle and begs her not to accept, but she will not be dissuaded. Reluctantly, he leaves to return home, and she enters the castle.

It is beautiful beyond belief. Marble tables, gold chandeliers, and all that she was promised. She is waited on by the best servants; her food, her clothing, her furniture, everything is more than she could wish for.

She is happy here . . . . but the happiest time of all is when she eats her meals with the man who spoke to her in the garden. He always stays behind a gold embroidered screen so that she can keep her promise never to look on him. Day by day she grows more anxious to know him and to care for him. She begins to look forward every day to the times when they will be together.

One afternoon, when they have been having a long talk over their afternoon tea, he tells her that he cares for her a great deal and wants her to marry him and live with him forever. She wants to accept immediately, because she has grown to love him dearly, but he says that before she makes up her mind, she must see him as he really is. He asks her to come to the great hall just before sunset, and he will show himself to her for the first time.

She is concerned, but she is sure that no matter what he looks like, she will still love him. She arrives at the hall. Slowly, he steps out from behind his gold embroidered screen. Shocked, she sees that he is not a man at all, but a beast. Not even a beast really. His ears are that of one animal, his mouth a different animal, his tail another, his hands and feet still another. He is unbelievably hideous. She runs to get away from this beast, but he calls after her to stay and be his wife, or he will surely die . . . . . Although she is a loving person, and although this creature has touched her heart, the sight of him is more than she can bear . . . . . She races to the castle door . . . . . Just as she opens it, she hears a pitiful cry. She turns to see that the beast has fallen to the floor . . . . She knows that he is dying . . . . . Only her love and willingness to stay and marry this beast will save him from death.

She sees him there on the floor . . . . . She is torn between her great love and her overwhelming desire to run away from this ugly beast . . . . . What will she do? You have one minute of time to see what she does and what will happen next. Begin. (Wait one minute)

Now bring this Journey to an end. And come back to this room, feeling the chair that you are sitting on and the floor under your feet . . . .

GROUNDING
In just a minute, I want you to open your eyes and write the ending to this story, the ending that you just saw happen. Start your writing from where the youngest daughter was at the door ready to run away, and the beast was on the floor dying. Write what happened next. Write it all down, so that someone can see the same pictures you saw. If you finish early, you may use the crayons and paper to illustrate any pictures that you saw as the story unfolded. If there are any questions, raise your hand. Without talking, ready, begin.

While the students are writing, go around and give encouragement for writers to communicate their mind pictures. This writing activity will take longer than the Grounding Activities up until now. Allow plenty of time for students to get their whole stories down on paper.

♣ **Create a Myth**

SHARING
Collect the story endings and read them to the class. Students can acknowledge authorship if they wish, or remain anonymous. Schedule this activity for the following day because this exercise is long.

EVALUATION
Continue to use the check, plus, or minus system, grading for effort only.

PHAETON AND APOLLO

MATERIALS NEEDED
For Each Student
Lined paper and pencils for writing, crayons and unlined paper for drawing, blindfold.

PREPARATION
- Tell students to get ready for a mind movie.
- Distribute materials. Explain that, as before, you will read a story up to a point, and then they will finish it.
- Dim lights as a signal to put on blindfolds or close eyes.

RELAXATION
Put your feet flat on the floor.... and shake out the tension from your shoulders and arms and hands.... Place your hands on your desktop....Take several deep breaths.... all the way in.... and all the way out.....and in.... feeling the oxygen traveling down to your legs and knees the toes... and out..... And once more all the way in, this time sending the oxygen into your throat and head and brain... and all the way out....

Now see yourself as a tree planted firmly in a meadow.... You can feel your roots going deep into the earth to support you and bring you moisture.... Feel the strength and support that these roots give you ..... You can feel your trunk straight and strong, holding you perfectly upright, to help you stay healthy and balanced... Moisture flows up your trunk from your roots, life-giving water.....

You can feel your branches spreading to the sun.... And you can feel the sun pouring its energy down on your leaves....The leaves soak up the sun's light, growing warmer and full of energy from the sun . . . . Allow yourself to enjoy this feeling of being a tree . . . . . with the sun's energy coming into you from your upturned leaves and the earth's strength and energy supporting you from below . . . . . And take one more deep breath, all the way in . . . . and all the way out . . . .

VISUALIZATION

Today on your Journey you will go back long ago and far away to a small village in ancient Greece. Phaeton, a handsome young boy, just about your age, lives alone with his mother, whom he loves and honors.

But as much as he loves his mother, he cannot help but miss having a father. His friends and schoolmates often tease him, saying that his father could not have loved him or his mother if he ran away from them.

His mother tells him that this is not true. His father loved her very much, and would love him, too, if only he could, but his father was not a mortal. He is Apollo, one of the gods, and gods are not allowed to live with mortals, even if they fall in love with one. The gods must live together on Mount Olympus, where they can watch over the human race.

Apollo has a particularly important job. He pulls the sun across the sky every day in a golden chariot drawn by seven immortal horses. His work brings light to the world, allowing the crops to grow and the earth to flourish. He could not possibly leave that vital work to come and live in a small house in an insignificant village.

The next time Phaeton's friends taunt him about his missing father, he tells them his mother's story. They laugh. They do not believe that Phaeton is the son of a god. They all know that Apollo is the god who pulls the fiery sun's chariot across the skies. Phaeton could not possibly be the son of the powerful god. Phaeton is embarrassed and angry at their disbelief. He decides to do something that will prove to them that he is truly the son of Apollo.

For several days he thinks about how to prove that Apollo is his father. Finally, he thinks of a plan. He decides to visit his father and ask to drive the sun's chariot across the sky. If his friends saw him driving the chariot that pulls the sun, they would know the truth of his words.

✣ **Create a Myth**

Phaeton travels down dusty roads, past poor homes . . . . . and rich homes . . . . . He stops and eats lunch under some olive trees, tasting the sweet bread and yellow cheese . . . . . At a well nearby, he pulls up water to drink and to wash off the dust of his travels . . . . . .

Soon after lunch, the path brings him to the foot of Mount Olympus, the home of the gods . . . It stretches high above.

The way to the palace of the Sun is steep and awesome, but he is young and strong, and determined to succeed . . . . . Finally he sees the palace in front of him . . . . .

As he approaches, the silver doors open to reveal a huge hall. The light from within is almost more than he can bear . . . . . The light is coming from the throne at the end of the hall, a throne made of gold encrusted with diamonds, and shining almost as brightly as the sun itself . . . . . Seated on this magnificent throne is Apollo. He is robed in deepest purple and crowned with rubies and amethysts.

Apollo instantly recognizes his son and makes him welcome . . . . He asks Phaeton why he came on this long, hard journey. Phaeton explains the trouble that he had with his friends, and tells him that he has a favor to ask. Out of his deep love for his son, Apollo grants him any wish that he might have. Phaeton asks to drive the sun chariot across the sky.

Apollo is thunderstruck. He begs Phaeton to reconsider, ask him anything but that. Driving the sun's chariot is beyond the power of a mere mortal. The horses are almost too much for even Apollo to control. And if the chariot gets out of control, it will go too low and scorch the earth, setting homes and fields on fire. If it goes too high, it will burn the heavens and the homes of the gods, and the earth will be left to freeze.

Even if Phaeton could keep the chariot on its course, there are terrible monsters which must be avoided: the wild bull, the archer, the lion, the scorpion, and the crab. It is dangerous beyond understanding.

But, there is nothing else Phaeton wants as much as this one favor. His friends will know beyond a doubt that he is the child of Apollo if he drives the sun's chariot through the skies . . . . .

Once more Apollo begs his son to change his mind. He says that if Phaeton insists, he must keep his promise, but he will grant any other wish if Phaeton will just release him from his pledge. Phaeton knows that his father is right about the dangers of the journey, but the sky beckons, and he remembers the taunts of his friends. What will he decide?

You have exactly one minute of time, to see what Phaeton decides and what will happen next. Begin. (Wait exactly one minute.)

Now bring the Journey to an end . . . . .Use your magic wand if you need it . . . . Come back to the classroom now, feeling your feet on the floor and your chair supporting you . . . . .

GROUNDING
In just a minute I will ask you to open your eyes. When it is time, I want you to write down what happened in your part of the story. Start at the place where Phaeton makes his decision about whether to insist on driving the sun's chariot across the sky. Write down everything that happened or was said from that moment on. If you finish early, illustrate your writing with pictures of what you saw.

If you have any questions, please raise your hand. Ready; begin.

This grounding activity will take quite a while for some students, as they will have a lot to write. Be sure to allow enough time. You can circulate and encourage the writing that clearly tells others about the writer's mental images.

SHARING
Collect and read the endings to the class. Students may or may not wish to acknowledge their authorship. This part of the activity will run over the hour allotted, and so may need to be finished the next day.

EVALUATION
I grade this on the check, plus, minus system for effort.

✤ **Create a Myth**

PANDORA'S BOX

MATERIALS NEEDED
For Each Student
Lined paper and pencils, unlined paper and crayons, blindfold.

PREPARATION
- Tell students they will be finishing another story today, and to get their mind movie ready to go.
- Distribute materials.
- Dim lights as a signal to close eyes or put on blindfolds.

RELAXATION
Please see that your feet are placed flat on the floor . . . . shake out your shoulders, arms, and hands . . . . . and place your hands on your desktop . . . Begin to relax as you take a good, deep breath all the way in . . . . and all the way out . . . . . .

Today we are going to use our tension dial once again. Breathe quietly for a moment, noticing the degree of tension you are holding in your body today . . . . . You may notice that you have greater amounts of tension in some parts of your body than in others . . . . . For now, do not try to change this, but just observe it . . . . notice how much tension you are holding today . . . . . Let's call your present level of tension 5.

Now I'd like you to visualize a tension control dial that goes from 0 to 10. Right now you can see that the dial is set at five. Turn the dial up to 6 . . . slightly increasing your level of tension . . . . . And then turn it up to 7 . . . . Now let it slip back to 6 . . . . and to 5 . . . . and then down to 4 . . . . Let it go even lower, to 3 . . . .

Now let's slowly increase the tension, going up to 4 . . . . to 5 . . . . to 6 . . . . to 7 . . . . to 8 . . . . And then let it go back down, sliding down the scale from 8 to 7 . . . . to 6 . . . . 5 . . . . then to 4 . . . . . down to 3 . . . . and 2 . . . . then to 1 . . . . and let your tension go all the way down to zero.

Now that your tension dial is set at zero, I want you to notice that you have another dial. This one also goes from 0 - 10, but instead of tension, this dial regulates your clear energy, or alertness. This dial

112

is set at 5 . . . . and we are going to turn in down just to 4 . . . . and you will feel slightly less full of clear energy, slightly less alert. Now turn the dial back to where you were, feeling more alert, and clear, but still keeping your tension dial at zero . . . . You can be very relaxed, yet still feel your own clear energy and alertness.

Leaving the tension dial at zero, turn the clear energy dial up to 6 . . . . feeling more good, clear energy, and then to 7 . . . . Now let it go back to 6, and then to 5, where you started.

Feel that blend of relaxation of energy . . . . Now let the clear energy dial go gently up again to 6 . . . . to 7 . . . . and to 8 . . . . to 9 and to 10 . . . . Feeling very relaxed and very alert at the same time, filled with a good, clear energy. Now let's begin today's Journey.

VISUALIZATION

We are going to go long ago and far away to a time when the earth is inhabited by children alone. Even the earth is young and beautiful. There is no disease, no death, no disappointment. The children are happy all of the time. They dance . . . . . they sing . . . . . they play in the meadows and streams . . . . . they pick the fruit off the trees for their food . . . . . and in these long ago times the fruit grows all the year around, for there is no winter to end the growing season.

Today we are going to the house of a boy named Epimetheus. See his house at the edge of a meadow . . . . . Epimetheus is wishing for a companion. He asks the gods to send him someone to keep him company.

The gods hear his wish and decide to send Pandora to him. She is a lovely and gracious young girl who is pleased to hear that she will be the companion for the kind boy, Epimetheus. When she is ready to go, Mercury, with his winged cap and winged feet, comes to fly her through the air to her new home.

Under Mercury's arm she can't help but notice a very large and very interesting box. She is curious about what could be in this box, and so are you. But one can't bother the gods by asking them a lot of questions, so she decides that it is probably a gift for Epimetheus, and she will wait until she reaches his home to find out what it is.
Mercury picks her up as if she were no heavier than a pillow of goose down.

♣ **Create a Myth**

Gently he flies her over the tree tops and house tops . . . . . over the cows and sheep . . . . . over the lakes and streams . . . . . over the children happily playing at their games . . . . .

Soon you notice that Mercury is descending . . . . . . and there is a lovely little house that seems to be their destination . . . . . They touch the earth once more and Epimetheus comes out of the house, greeting Pandora and making her feel welcome at once . . . . . Mercury deposits the large box inside the house and makes ready to leave.

Pandora stops him, asking about the box. "Oh yes," answers Mercury. "I meant to tell you about that. Pandora, you and Epimetheus are to keep this box and guard it. But you are never to open it. Whatever happens, do not open the box."

Now Pandora does not know what is in this box, or why the gods have given the box to her, but you must know the answers to those questions.

The gods were very angry with the human race. They didn't like to see all the children running around, living life as happily as the gods themselves. So they got together to figure out a way to punish humanity.

They decided to gather up a collection of nasty little black creatures called Troubles. There was one called Death, one called Jealousy, and one called Hatred. Lies, Cheating, Disease, Guilt and Anger all were gathered up by the gods like so many buzzing insects, and all were put into the box.

But the Gods began to feel a little sorry that they were bringing so much evil to the human race. They decided that at the very bottom of the box they would put a lovely, rainbow-winged creature named Hope. So in went Hope, last of all, where she took refuge in the corner at the bottom of the box. Then the gods gave the box to Mercury, who, in turn, gave it to Pandora. Mercury and all the other gods were sure that Pandora would not long be able to keep from looking inside the box.

Ignorant of what the gods had planned, at first Pandora is hardly bothered by the presence of the box. There are new friends to meet, and new places to see . .

. . . As the days go by though, she begins to notice the box more and more. She begins to spend hours looking at it . . . . . wondering what treasure could possibly be contained inside . . . . . If it comes from the gods, it must be something wonderful . . . . . clothes of gold, or jewels . . . . . Why did Mercury give it to her if he didn't really want her to open it? . . . Perhaps, she thinks, Mercury wanted to test her bravery . . . Perhaps he hoped that she would have the courage to open it . . .

Oh, a hundred excuses run through her head, urging her to open the box.

*While Epimetheus and the other children are out playing, she sits by the box, running her fingers over its surface. Notice what the box is made of . . . . . Look at how it is fastened . . . . . It could easily be undone and opened . . . .
One day, as Pandora sits near the box, overcome with curiosity, a tiny voice seems to come from inside of the box, saying, "Pandora, let us out. Let us out. We want to play with you."*

She is amazed. She thinks that they may be little elves, or perhaps caterpillars and butterflies. She cannot bear to think of living things trapped inside a dark old box. Her fingers go to the clasp, and almost without her effort, the clasp is undone all by itself.

Instantly, she regrets what she has done, and tries to fasten the box together again, but she cannot. It is as if a part of the clasp were missing. She knows that when Epimetheus comes in from play and sees the box unfastened, he will think that she has already opened the lid and peeked inside.

Pandora decides that if Epimetheus will think she has peeked inside the box, then she might as well go ahead and do it. Her hand goes to the lid of the box. She pauses, hearing the children playing outside. The sunshine seems to be saying, "Why bother about that old box, Pandora? Come outside and play in the meadow with your friends."

Then she looks back at the box and thinks of the little voices inside, begging to be let out. She knows that if she does not open the box today, it will be there tomorrow and the next day and the next, always begging her to open it and end the suspense. (It's as if you knew where all your Christmas presents were hidden, but you weren't supposed to go and look.)

♣ Create a Myth

While she is trying to decide, Epimetheus comes into the house behind her. For a moment, at least, he doesn't make a move to stop her from opening the box. He stands quietly, watching to see what she will do.

Put yourself in Pandora's place, sitting by this box that is begging to be opened. What will you do?

You will have exactly one minute of time to watch and see what you will do, and what will happen next. Ready, begin. (Wait exactly one minute.)

Now bring this to a close, using your magic wand if you need to, to finish up anything that you would like . . . . And come back to this room, with the floor beneath your feet and your desk supporting you.

GROUNDING
Not yet, but in just a minute I want you to write down what happened. First tell whether the box was opened or not, and then tell what happened next. Write down everything that happened and everything that was said. If you finish early, you may illustrate your story with any pictures you saw in your mind's eye as the story unfolded. Do not talk until all of the work is done. If you have any questions, raise your hand and I will come to your desk. Ready; begin.

Circulate and encourage good writing. Remember that this activity will take quite a while for some of your students.

SHARING
You can collect the papers and read the endings, or ask for volunteers to read the endings, or pair up students and have them read their endings to each other.

EVALUATION
Grade on effort only, with the check, plus, minus system.

8 Image While You Read

RATIONALE
In a California State Title IVC project called Mind's Eye, there is considerable opinion that the formation of images in conjunction with reading the printed word is a key to comprehension and retention.

In an article in the *Journal of Educational Psychology*, Anderson and Hidde are quoted as saying:

"The ability of subjects to generate or use visual imagery in their attempt to comprehend written discourse is considered to be a central factor differentiating good from poor readers."

If we hope to turn poor readers into good readers, I believe that it is worth a concentrated effort to teach that poor reader to learn to visualize what he or she reads. We need to bring together the students' ability to visualize with their ability to decode, with the desired result that students begin to truly see and understand what they are reading. When students read with eagerness, laughing aloud in the funny parts, they become a part of the stories they read, learning about the nature of humanity and developing empathy for others as understanding and comprehension grows.

DESCRIPTION
Teachers guide small groups of students in reading. Then, each student describes in detail what he or she has visualized from that sentence. Later, students read a paragraph at a time, then a whole story. Always, the teacher asks for the images in detail.

PURPOSE
To transfer the skill of visualization to the printed word. Students develop the habit of making a detailed picture in their minds' eye for everything they read. They develop images for characters, settings, and action.

SCHEDULING
Time needed for each lesson: 60-80 minutes
Number of lessons: Ten.

❖ Image While You Read

TWO-WEEK PLAN FOR IMAGING WHILE YOU READ

MATERIALS NEEDED
For Each Student
A copy of a short story selection at a reading level below that of most of the students, and a blank 5" x 8" index card.

For The Teacher
A list of questions specially prepared for the story and an extra story in case the class finishes the first one before this plan is completed.

PREPARATION
- Find a good, very short (two to four page) story. It needs to be interesting, lending itself to lots of mental images, and it should be at least two grade levels below that of most of your students' reading ability. To avoid frustrating your low readers, select a story with little dialogue. Fairy tales work very well for this activity. "The Frog Prince," "The Fisherman and His Wife," "Tom Thumb's Travels," or "The Elves" from any collection of *Grimm's Fairy Tales*, are all good selections. From *Time for Fairy Tales Old and New* by Arbuthnot, you can use "Wippety Stouri," "The Fisherman and His Wife," "March and the Shepherd," "How Many Donkeys?" or "The Elephant's Child."
- Divide your class into groups of about six.
- Find or make enough copies of the story so that each student in a group has one.
- Divide your copy of the story into sections for use each day. This division will be based on timing considerations and will allow you to prepare questions for each day. Use the guide lines listed below in the Day One section to create your questions.
- Prepare seat work to be used while you meet with each small group for fifteen to twenty minutes each day.

DAY ONE
Step One: Meet with your small groups one at a time. Direct the students to place their index cards under the sentence being read. This keeps students from reading ahead while you are discussing images. Have one student read the first sentence aloud. Now, give all the students a turn to tell you about their mental pictures of that sentence. Students need not shut their eyes unless they prefer to do so. By now, most students will be able to visualize with their eyes open. If someone has a problem, ask all students to close their eyes for a minute while you repeat the sentence, and the students look to see what appears in their imaginations.

Ask detailed questions about: setting, appearance of characters, feeling of characters, weather, colors, thoughts of characters, time of day, time frame of story, what odd words or names might mean, and predicated actions. You will spend ten or more minutes just on this one sentence.

EXAMPLE: "The boy ran wildly through the darkened streets."
  Setting: Is the boy in a city or village? Are the streets narrow or broad?
  Appearance of Characters: How is the boy dressed? How old is the boy? Is he rich or poor?
  Weather: What does the sky look like? Does it seem to be cold or hot?
  Colors: What color is the street? What colors are the boy's clothes?
  Thoughts of Characters: What do you suppose the boy is thinking?
  Time of Day: Is it dark or light? Where are the other people—are they in the street too, or in bed?
  Period of Story: Is this happening in modern times, or some other time?
  Predicated Actions: Do you think he will get where he is going? Do you suppose he is running from something, or running to catch or find something?

These are only suggestions. Notice that they take the student beyond what is said in the text. The questions are never about what is said, but about the image the student is creating from what is said.

When you first ask these questions, students may be reluctant to answer. This is largely because they are accustomed to having to justify their responses by pointing to the exact source on the page. Your most conscientious students may need the most encouragement, as they become comfortable with "making stuff up" that is not fully justified by the printed word.

♣ **Image While You Read**

You must accept all interpretations, whether they make sense to you or not. Point out how different everyone's pictures are. Later, your readers will bring their pictures closer to what the author had in mind, but let them come to that on their own. Encourage each student's individual point of view, so that each student is really doing the job of visualizing independently.

If some students' responses are really unsupported by the print, then when those students read the next sentence, ask them if their reading now changes their mental image. Ask why or why not. Let them do the job of aligning their images with the printed material.

Step Two: Ask students to move their index cards so that only the next sentence is showing. It is important to insist upon this; otherwise, some eager readers will read ahead and not be a part of your lesson. Have another student read the next sentence. Again, press each student for details about this next sentence. Sooner or later, prompted by your positive expectations, most students begin to see something.

This process is often a new experience for poor readers, as you are treating both your good and poor readers with identical respect and demands for performance. The low achievers are startled at first. Their traditional, "I don't know," is countered with your reply of, "Well, take a look and see. There is no right answer. I just want to know what you see." You make it nearly impossible for them to fail at this task, because any answer to "What color is the boy's shirt?" is a correct answer. As the poorer students realize that you expect them to come up with pictures just as good or better than those that the high-achievers generate, they usually begin to perform. Since there are no right or wrong pictures in this activity, or indeed in any of the previous activities, these visualizations give a fresh new start to students who are quite accustomed to having their efforts met with constant criticism.

Step Three: If you run out of time before you get to the third step, begin here on the second day. Repeat the process of reading one sentence at a time and then asking each student questions to stimulate visualization. Continue to use the index cards.

Next, have one student read all the sentences that have been read and discussed so far. This might only be three or four sentences altogether if you have explored them richly.

DAYS TWO AND THREE

Step Four: On the second day, repeat the activities of the first, continuing from where you left off the day before. Do the same on the third day as well. Continue to insist on the index card covering the unread material. Continue reminding your students of their purpose in this activity: to create rich images as they read.

DAYS FOUR, FIVE, AND SIX

Step Five: Continue with the same story, using the index card in the same manner, but now ask each student to read an entire paragraph before stopping to ask for the details of the student's visualization. You might finish your story about now. If you do, just go on to another brief and entertaining selection.

DAYS SEVEN, EIGHT, NINE, AND TEN

Continue as before, and expand reading to three or four paragraphs before stopping for discussion. It is not necessary to have a student reread the selection at the end of the twenty minute session. At this step, you can do that activity with your entire class, taking a much longer time for the questions so that every student is asked for some images. Or ask the students to respond on paper first, so that every student responds to every question.

EVALUATION

The work in this chapter helps most students make the transition to visualization from the printed word.

If someone needs additional practice, you might record an Extended Activity from Chapter 2 or 3, or give more practice along the guidelines in this chapter.

9
What Turtle?

DESCRIPTION
The class reads a story aloud together. As each section is read, the teacher quizzes students about the pictures they are creating to give life to the story.

PURPOSE
To reinforce further the skills of visualization while reading and to promote the habit of reading.

SCHEDULING
Time needed for each lesson: 30-40 minutes
Number of lessons: Two or three a week for two weeks. Then, one or two a week for several months, as needed.

RATIONALE
Students need to make a strong and permanent connection between visualizing and decoding. In Chapter 8, when guided, they learned to link the two skills. Now, they must make the link independently. This is accomplished by lengthening the time periods between which you question each student. Every few paragraphs, interrupt the story with questions about the details of their own personal pictures.

In previous chapters, you planted in your poorer readers the expectation that you will call on them and expect them to have a good answer. It is important that you continue to call on all students and probe in a positive way until each student visualizes from print.

PREPARATION
- Prepare a copy of the reading material.
- Tell students that they will read a story (or an article) together. They will use index cards in the way they have done before. Remind them not to read ahead.
- Tell them that they will be asked for answers to the kinds of questions that are not found in the text and will need to visualize in order to answer.
- Remind students that there are many right answers to the questions you will ask.
- Distribute materials. Have students number their papers for as many questions as you intend to ask.

VISUALIZATION

Call on various students to read as the rest of the class follows along, using the 5" x 8" index cards to keep from reading ahead.

Every few paragraphs, interrupt the story to ask for details of each student's visualization. Use the kinds of questions you have asked previously. Be sure to call on your slower readers at least as often as your top reader.

After asking each question, have students write their answers on paper. Then immediately discuss those answers. For complex scientific descriptions, you may need to stop and have your students draw their perceptions several times during the reading.

Read another paragraph or two, ask a question, record, discuss, and continue. During the discussion, if a student has no picture, have all the students shut their eyes while the material is reread by you or a student. Try to involve every student in the visualization process.

If you would rather discuss without the paper/pencil activity, be sure to use one of the Grounding Activities suggested below. Let your students know what that activity will be before they begin to read. In that way, your students will be tuned into the proper cues.

MATERIALS NEEDED
For Each Student
A good short story or non-fiction article, a 5" x 8" index card, and a sheet of lined paper. Science magazines and articles about nature are especially good resources for this activity.

For The Teacher
A list of questions that you have created about the story or article. Your questions should require students to answer beyond literal recall, prompting them to visualize in order to answer.

✤ **What Turtle?**

To involve every student, do not call on a student until you have given everyone time to think of an answer. Each student will be reviewing his visualization, building on it, and expecting to be called upon.

GROUNDING

If you do not choose to use the paper/pencil questions, grounding is needed for this activity because you may not have time to call on all students to tell their visualizations. Many images that students have created during the reading will not be translated into language, so a final grounding exercise is needed.

Your selection will depend on the nature of the material that you have selected for reading with your class. You will probably think of many other good activities to add to the list below. The criteria for inventing such activities should be:
- There is no right or wrong answer. This insures success for all who make the effort.
- The activity calls on the students' own pictures, not on the literal translation of the author's words.
- It is not too lengthy or it might discourage students from reading the next story they are assigned.
- Its completion does not depend on a student's ability to read more material independently, material that they might not yet comprehend.

SUGGESTED GROUNDING ACTIVITIES
- Students draw a picture of each main character. Below the picture they write the character's name, and seven words that describe the character.
- Materials needed: ten sheets of tagboard, or ten large sheets of butcher paper. Ten students each write just one important event from the story on each of the ten sheets of tagboard. Arbitrarily put a number from one to ten on each board. Display the tagboard sheets so they are visible to the class. Each student, at his own desk, now lists the proper order of these events on his paper, using the number code on the tagboard sheets.

Next, the class works together to put the ten boards in their proper order. Someone from the class can then retell the story using the boards as reminders. This activity offers practice with sequencing.

- After the class has read and discussed the whole selection, the teacher names one of the main story characters and asks questions about this character. Students record their answers on paper. The questions should be about details that were not stated in the story itself, such as height, age, hobbies, clothing, anything that was not specified. After each question, the students write down what they think. Then class members share what they wrote and why. This sharing could be done with the whole group or with learning partners.
- After the story, you might ask some predictive questions to help your students develop a character more fully. Here are a few sample ideas:
  > Do you think Peter Pan would rather kill Captain Hook, or use magic to turn him into a decent person. Why?
  >
  > Do you think Wendy would rather wear a fancy pink dress or blue jeans? Why?
  >
  > If little Red Riding Hood had a gun, do you think she would have shot the Big Bad Wolf when he tried to eat her? Why?
  >
  > If Goldilocks had found a pot of gold in the Three Bears' house, do you think she would have stolen it? Why?
  >
  > If Cinderella could have spoiled her sisters' ball gowns without getting caught or punished, do you think she would have done it? Why?
  >
  > Which of the characters in *The Lion, the Witch, and the Wardrobe* do you think will make the best parents when they grow up? Why?

Notice that while these questions sometimes have to do with moral judgments, I am not asking students what they think is the right thing to do, but rather what they think the character would do. This leads students to think in terms of characters that have certain tendencies and will often act in predictable ways.

- Each student picks one character from the story, writes the name of the character, and then lists details about that character: physical appearance, clothes, likes and dislikes, age, personality, strengths, and weaknesses. You might furnish a list of characteristics for the first few times that students do this activity, to help them to think about the character from many angles.

- If the setting is an important part of the story, the students might draw or write a description of how they visualize the setting. They should not be allowed to consult their story again as they do this, or they will be tempted to repeat the author's words. Remember, there are many right answers.

- In a science article, it might be appropriate to draw the process described. For example, if they read an article describing how a glacier carves a mountainside, they could draw a picture of it. If there is already a picture in the article, they could draw the glacier from a different perspective, or in a different stage.

- When a building, a contraption, or a vehicle is important to the story, students can draw it. Unless the object is very clearly described, the students can reread the description after you have given the assignment and before they begin to draw. Then the book should be set aside as the students add their own details to the author's description. Accuracy is not as important as imagination, but the imagination should be built upon the text's foundation.

SHARING
This is accomplished during the class discussion. If you do some of the grounding activities, they might also be shared with the whole class or with learning partners or groups.

EVALUATION
If the paper/pencil activity is used, it can be graded with a check, plus, or minus for effort. Some of the grounding activities lend themselves to similar evaluation.

Remember the main point of these exercises is to guide your students to create a picture in their minds, using only the printed word as stimulus. It is not terribly important that at this point the pictures accurately reflect the author's intention. Students' pictures will grow more and more accurate as they become practiced in visualizing their reading material. As a result, their comprehension and understanding usually increases markedly.

10
Imaging in Content Areas

RATIONALE
In much the same way that it is possible to read a story without creating any pictures for the characters and action, students can read their science, social studies, or math books without 'seeing' what the author is explaining or describing.

By giving students the tool of visualization to comprehend factual material, you can greatly assist their ability to learn from what they read on their own. In order to teach this skill, at first we exaggerate it, asking the student to visualize each detail. Later, they can use this skill wherever it is appropriate, especially in new or difficult material.

There are two ways to work with visualization in the content areas. The first is to have the students read a selection and then visualize and answer questions. This technique is described in Chapter 9, "What Turtle?" In another approach, you write out a script that takes students through a process such as glaciation or a trip in a rocket ship to the sun. Let's first look at the way you would have students read and visualize.

DESCRIPTION
The techniques outlined in Chapter 9 will be repeated, this time using material out of the content areas.

PURPOSE
To teach students to use their visualizing skills to increase comprehension as they read in the content areas.

SCHEDULING
Time needed for each lesson: 30-45 minutes
Number of lessons: Five
(One daily for one week; then, one per week, as needed, scheduled in the content area time period.)

❖ Imaging in Content Areas

MATERIALS NEEDED
For Each Student
A reading selection from a content area such as math, science, or social studies, and a 5" x 8" index card to cover the unread material. Optional: a piece of lined paper and a pencil.

For The Teacher
A list of questions based on the selection and designed to take students beyond mere facts and into visualization.

READ AND VISUALIZE

PREPARATION
- Find a selection of which you would like students to increase their understanding.
- Create your questions. Examples are given below.
- Distribute materials. Have students number the paper with as many questions as you anticipate asking.
- Tell students that the questions you will ask them will go beyond what is on the printed page, and that they will need to make mind pictures in order to answer.

VISUALIZATION QUESTIONS
You may do this activity in small groups, or with the entire class. Read one sentence or one or two paragraphs depending on the level of difficulty. Then ask many questions in order to encourage a great deal of visualization. Read a second sentence, asking if it changes the perceptions from the first sentence, and instructing students to visualize further. Have each student respond first on paper and then orally, to get maximum participation, unless, later, you may find it unnecessary and interfering with the process.

Science Example:
Read from a science book: "Many forces can change the shape of a mountain."
Ask students: "Close your eyes and visualize a force that is changing the shape of a mountain. Now, what does the mountain look like: What is the force? What does it look like? Now, how has the mountain changed?" (They could write about this or draw before answering aloud.)
Read the next sentence: "But one of the most powerful, and relatively fast-acting, is the glacier."
Ask students: "Close your eyes and see a glacier changing the shape of the mountain. What color is the glacier? How much of the mountain does it cover? Is it moving or still? How is it changing the mountain's shape?"

Read the next sentence: "A glacier is formed by falling snow which builds up year after year. Eventually the snow on the bottom is pressed so hard that it turns to ice."

Ask students: "Close your eyes, and watch the snow fall year after year. See the pressure of the snow on top build up until the bottom layers of snow turn into ice. About how much snow do you see falling each year? Show me with your hands if you can. Are the snow and ice the same color? Is the ice clear or opaque? How thick do you see the layers getting before the pressure is enough to begin to form ice?"

This is not a technique to use when you need to "cover the material." It is very slow. You might only discuss two or three sentences the first day. But remember that your objective is not so much that students learn this particular material, but that they learn to generate pictures in their minds for the words found on a textbook page. And, even though your objective may not be the mastery of this particular subject, visualizing in this way does insure a thoroughness of understanding. You may find it worthwhile to use this method when introducing new or difficult material.

Math Example:
Students read a math problem: "John drove fifty-three miles in his parents' car. Sally drove only twenty-five in her car. Susan drove thirty-six miles in her car on the same road as the others. When they all stopped, which two people were closer to each other?"

Say: "Now, I want you to get a picture of what is happening here. Please draw a picture of John, Sally, and Susan all in the same place. Next, draw a guess of the distances each drove and label it with the correct number of miles each drove. Now, looking at your picture, figure out how you can tell which two are closer to each other."

Making pictures for math problems, either in your mind's eye or on paper, is a powerful tool for making sense of all those words.

♣ **Imaging in Content Areas**

MATERIALS NEEDED
For Each Student
Materials you have chosen for the Grounding Activity.

For The Teacher
The script that you have written.

VISUALIZATION JOURNEY

To help students understand a process that it is difficult or complex, you may wish to create a visualization so that they can experience the process as if they were a part of it. You can send them out into space to appreciate the size and wonder of the universe. Or, you can have them become a seed, floating through the air, landing in warm moist soil, waiting for rainfall, sending out tentative roots, until it has fully matured. The following example teaches students about the digestive system.

RELAXATION
Take your students through any relaxation activities that you like, or just ask them to center and take a few deep, slow breaths. Be sure to tell them to close their eyes.

VISUALIZATION
Today I want you to imagine yourself being a bite of carrot. Your greatest and only desire is to nourish the child who is going to eat you. You are not sure how you are going to provide this nourishment. You know that you cannot do it all by yourself, and you wonder what will happen to you as you go into a mouth and down to a stomach. Remember that you are a carrot, and not a person. You have no sense of pain or discomfort. Everything you experience is going to be interesting and unusual, but it will not cause you discomfort.

At the beginning of this Journey, from being a bite of a carrot to turning into a burst of pure energy, you find yourself inside a mouth . . . . You slide over the soft tongue . . . feeling the saliva gliding you along . . . just like ice skating across the tongue . . . And now you bump into some very hard teeth . . . crunch . . . you are being chewed and mixed with the saliva to form a soupy mixture . . . see how it feels to become a soupy liquid . . . sloshing around the teeth and the tongue in the dark mouth . . . . .

Oops, suddenly you are pushed down a tube . . . it is the esophagus . . . you slip and slide as muscles push you down in a wave-like motion . . . . . So this is peristalsis . . . As each wave of the peristalsis comes, you go down a little further. You had been wondering if you would fall all the way to the stomach, but this isn't at all like falling . . . it is a gentle, wave-like pushing . . . as if you were standing in the ocean and being gently nudged along by the shore-line waves.

Now you land, splash, in a sea of stomach juices . . . . You look around and find yourself in a cavern that is about half-full of liquid. You know that these stomach acids and juices are there to finish the job of breaking you down so that you can achieve your goal of becoming more and more liquid.

Now you feel yourself slipping little by little into a new tube . . the small intestine . . . You can't move by yourself, having no legs or arms, but you can feel the peristalsis gently shoving you along down the tube of the small intestine . . . . Your carrot-ness is slowly disappearing . . . instead you are becoming a pile of carbohydrates, fats, and proteins . . . . ready to be turned into pure energy.

But you wonder how this will happen . . . You are still in this small intestine tube . . . How can you get out? . . You know that you need to get into the bloodstream and to the cells of this child's body. You want to feed muscle cells, heart cells, brain cells . . . Maybe you can be the burst of energy that wins the race, or solves the long division problem . . . . But how?

Then you begin to feel yourself drawn, almost sucked toward the walls of this tube you are in . . . . And you notice that the walls of this small intestine are very bumpy . . . . You feel yourself being pulled in between the bumps . . . The bumps are called villi. You swim and swirl in between these bumps . . . . You slide down them . . . . You are having as much fun as a kid on a waterslide.

After a time, you feel yourself pulled in between these villi . . . . You realize that you have been broken down into such a fine soup by the stomach acids and juices that you are going to be pulled right through the wall of this intesintal tube . . . . . You come close to the base of one of the villi . . . .closer . . . and closer . . . and instead of bumping into it, you dissolve right through the wall as if it weren't there at all . . . . .

And here you are, in a whole new place . . . . Everything is red . . . . . You are surrounded by warm, red liquid that is traveling along like a river . . . . .You are floating gently along in all of this redness . . . . .You realize that you are now in the child's bloodstream. . . . . You enjoy being moved along by this life-giving liquid . . . . You know that you are now on your way right to a cell in this child's body. Any second now you will be picked up by one of the muscle cells, or heart cells, or brain cells, and be instantly turned into a burst of energy . . . You can hardly wait . . . .

Now I would like you to come back to this classroom and feel the floor under your feet . . . . feel the desk you are sitting in . . . .Begin to stretch, and when you are ready, open your eyes.

GROUNDING

Your choice of a grounding activity will vary with the content, your interest, and creativity. A few of the many ways to ground in some of the content areas follow:

Writing:
After reading a description of families leaving their homes to be part of the Westward movement, students could make a list of what they would take with them for survival and for pleasure.

After experiencing a visualization journey into the solar system and the universe, students could write a list of ten words that described how they felt out there.

Drawing:
After reading a selection describing the discovery of gold at Sutter's Mill, students could collaborate on a mural depicting the event.

After reading a description of one of our planets, students could draw their perception of it with crayons, and cover the drawing with a black wash.

Dramatizing: After reading a description of the Boston Tea Party, students could act out the event.

While you are describing the transformation of a small seed into a large tree, primary students could pretend to be the growing seed in all of its stages.

Dancing:
After reading a description of how atoms join to become molecules, students could form groups that combine to become atoms, and then the atomic groups could join with others to form molecules.

After reading about the behavior of an animal, primary students could become that animal, and dance out the behaviors as you retell the story.

Models:
After reading a description of the windmill and dike systems in the Netherlands, students could make a three-dimensional model.

After reading of an event at a historical site, such as Washington crossing the Delaware, students could make a clay model of the scene.

Language:
Merely expressing a concept or image orally can be grounding by itself. Therefore any time that you provide the opportunity for *each student* to express his or her image verbally, you are creating a grounding exercise. If your group or class is reading aloud together and you ask specific questions of each student about each image, the imaging and grounding are both present.

When you take the option of having students write down each answer before you discuss it, there is grounding. Grounding also occurs when students sit in pairs and tell each other what they see after each visualization question from you.

SHARING
This will vary with your grounding activity.

EVALUATION
By looking at students' written answers, or listening as they discuss, you will be able to assess their progress in their ability to visualize from the content area material. In grading, mark the paper/pencil work or the other grounding activity with a check, plus, minus system based on effort.

11
Vocabulary Books

DESCRIPTION
The teacher will choose five related words that students are not likely to know. They will image one word a day and draw what they visualize. At week's end they will write one sentence, correctly using all the vocabulary words.

PURPOSE
To develop skills and strategies for comprehending new words encountered in independent reading. Students will play with the meaning of words and perceive new new words as interesting puzzles.

SCHEDULING
Time needed for each lesson: 30-40 minutes
Number of lessons: One, plus suggestions for nine more to be created by the teacher.

RATIONALE
We do not increase vocabularies by merely memorizing lists of words and their meanings. To become familiar with a word, it must be experienced in both a right- and a left-brained way. Pleasure is one of the emotions that helps us remember an incident or a word. Because these vocabulary books present words through a pleasant experience, and because they keep the words in the students' attention for a span of time, it is highly likely that these words will become part of your students' vocabularies.

The major benefits of this approach are two: it is another way to keep students practicing visualization so that their reading will remain enriched, and it is a way to teach students new word attack skills when encountering unfamiliar material.

Students will be more likely to imagine some possible meaning for new words, meaning that will make the most sense in the sentence where they see it. This is the essence of the powerful skill of using context clues to determine word meanings. By encouraging imagination in each encounter with a new word, we train students to use context clues.

Vocabulary Books ♣

PREPARATION
- Distribute the materials.
- Create the booklets. To make the vocabulary booklets, tell your students to follow these steps:

1. Place the three white papers on top of the construction paper.
2. Fold the papers in half horizontally, with the construction paper on the outside.
3. Staple the papers at the fold.
4. Open the booklet and write the title, "Vocabulary Book," and name on the first white page, which is the title page.
5. Turn the page and begin numbering the pages from 1 to 10. The last white page, at the end of the book, will not be numbered.

After the first experience, students can make the booklets without your help.

- Choose five related vocabulary words that your students are unlikely to know.
- Explain to students that they will be working in their books for a week, adding one word each day. You will ask them to visualize words that they probably will not know, and to create a vivid mental picture for each word.
- Write "precipice," the word for the day, on the chalkboard and have the students write it at the top of their page number one. Tell them that they will be drawing their mental picture of the word on that page only. Page number two will have another use. Each day of the vocabulary book activities, the word for the day will be written on the odd-numbered pages.

RELAXATION
Optional.

MATERIALS NEEDED
For Each Student
Three 8 1/2" x 11" sheets of unlined paper and one 8 1/2" x 11" sheet of colored construction paper.

135

♣ **Vocabulary Books**

Day One
VISUALIZATION
As you close your eyes today and relax . . . clear your mind . . . and let your thoughts and concerns float away. . . . I want you to imagine an ocean . . . water in every direction . . . . Everywhere there is ocean . . . Notice its color . . . Notice the smells . . . . Notice the sounds . . . . Notice if the air is warm or cold . . . . . Notice whether the waves are gentle or high . . . . Notice what the sky looks like . . . . See if the sun is shining or if there are clouds . . . . . Notice if you see anything else in the sky today . . . . . and notice if you see anything on the ocean . . . .

Now look toward the shore . . . . As you move a little closer to the shore to see it better, you notice a high precipice right at the edge of the shore. Take a look at the precipice. What color is it ? . . . . What is it made of ? . . . . Do you see anything on it, or is it empty?

GROUNDING
In just a minute I will ask you to open your eyes and represent what you have been seeing. You can draw anything of what you saw, the ocean, the sky, the waves, anything at all, but be sure to make the precipice a part of your picture. It doesn't matter what you think the precipice is, or what you think it looks like. There are no right or wrong answers in this part of today's work. I want you to use your imagination so that no two people will draw precipices that look alike . . . . Ready, open your eyes and draw, using only page one. Do not draw on page two, as we will need that for another purpose in just a few minutes.

SHARING
Share by asking for volunteers to show what they drew and what they think a precipice is. The teacher may want to ask students for a show of hands to see how many had the same idea as at least a few of their classmates. Some may think it is an animal, some a boat, or something else.

See if the class can come to a consensus on the true meaning of 'precipice.' At the end of the discussion, ask a student to find and read the definition in the dictionary. By this time, students are very eager to see who is right.

When everyone has discovered the true meaning of precipice, have all of the students either draw or write this meaning on page two, which faces their earlier drawing. Do not allow dictionaries open for copying at this time; students should use their own words.

Day Two
PREPARATION
- Distribute materials.
- Write the word for the day on the board: "sloop." Have the students write it on page three of their books.

RELAXATION
Optional.

VISUALIZATION
Close your eyes, relax . . . and get comfortable . . . . we are going back to the ocean again . . . . Notice how the water looks today . . . . See the color . . . . . See the waves . . . . Notice if they are slow or fast . . . . high or low . . . . . Now listen to the sounds here at the ocean today . . . . and feel the air. Notice if it is warm or cold . . . . Is there wind, or is the air calm ? . . . . Notice the sky . . . Are there clouds or sunshine, or both ? . . . . Is there anything flying in the air .? . . . Now notice the ocean smells . . . . What colors do you see in the sky today? . . . . On the ocean? . . . .

Now you look over to the shore and see the precipice. Is there anything on top of the precipice today? . . . . . How big is it? . . . . .

Look back at the ocean once again. . . . . On the ocean today you are going to see a sloop. The sloop is gliding along the surface of the water . . . . . Notice whether it is moving fast or slowly . . . . . See what it looks like, gliding over the water . . . . . What color is it? . . . Does it make any sounds? . . . . . See if it is going straight or if it turns left or right . . . . . Watch and see what happens to the sloop as the waves touch it . . . . . Notice the size of the sloop compared to the waves . . . . .

✤ Vocabulary Books

GROUNDING

In just a minute I will ask you to open your eyes and represent some of what you saw today in your mind's eye. You may include anything of what you saw, but be sure to include the sloop. Remember that there is no right or wrong answer about this. I want to see what your imagination produced when you heard the word 'sloop.' On page three, please represent what you think a sloop is. You can include other things in the picture as well. Remember, do not draw on page four, only on page three. Begin.

SHARING

As before, ask a student to find and read the definition in the dictionary. Then, have all the students draw or write the word's true meaning on page four.

Day Three
PREPARATION:
- Distribute materials.
- Write the words for the day: "craggy rocks."

RELAXATION
Optional.

VISUALIZATION

Please close your eyes, relax, and get ready for our Journey . . . I want you to go back again to the ocean. There you see the precipice . . . and the sloop . . . . . See how the sloop is doing today . . . . . Are the ocean waves gentle, or is the sloop being tossed around? . . . . . What about the sky? . . . . . What about the air? . . . . . What sounds do you hear on the ocean today? . . . . . Notice the colors of the ocean . . . . . The colors of the sky . . . . . the shore . . . . . the color of the sloop and its sails . . . . .

Now I want you to look toward the shore again. Today you are going to look for craggy rocks by the edge of the ocean. Some of them are in the ocean, and some are near the precipice . . . . . What do these craggy rocks look like? . . . Are they small or large . . . . . What shape are they? . . . . . What colors do you see? . . . . Does anything grow on the craggy rocks? . . . . . How many do you see? . . . . .

GROUNDING

Today, when you open your eyes you will draw the craggy rocks. You can include anything else you want, but be sure to show the craggy rocks. Draw only on page five. Open your eyes and begin.

SHARING

As before, refer a student to the dictionary and share the meaning with the class. Then ask them to draw or write the true meaning for 'craggy rocks' on page six.

Day Four
PREPARATION
- Distribute materials.
- Write the word for the day: "obstacles."

VISUALIZATION

Please close your eyes. Today, as you get ready for your Journey, you are going back once more to the ocean . . . . . Enjoy the sounds of the ocean, and the smells . . . . . and the wind. Is it soft or strong today? . . . . . Are there any birds or fish . . . . . Notice the color and texture of the water . . . . . What is the sky like today? . . . . . Can you feel the warmth of the sun? . . . . .

Now you look toward the shore and see the precipice and the craggy rocks below. You notice the sloop sailing through the waters . . . . . What are the waves like today? . . . . . What kind of a time is the sloop having? . . . . . . Again look toward the shore, and notice that there are some obstacles in the water. Some of the obstacles are quite large, but some are small and can hardly be noticed. The sloop is heading for these obstacles . . . . . What color are they? . . . . . What do you think they are made of? . . . . . How do you think they happen to be there? . . . . . . What do you think will happen to the sloop if she sails close to them? . . . . .

GROUNDING

In just a minute, you will open your eyes and represent what you have just created in your mind's eye. You may draw any part of the pictures you saw, but be sure to include the obstacles. I want to see what your imagination did with the word 'obstacles.' Draw only on page seven. Begin.

✤ **Vocabulary Books**

SHARING
As before, have someone look up and read the meaning in the dictionary. Then ask them to draw or write the true meaning of 'obstacles' on page eight.

Day Five
PREPARATION
- Distribute materials.
- Write "careening" on the board.

RELAXATION
Optional.

VISUALIZATION
Close your eyes, please. Today, we are going back to the ocean for one more visit. We will see all of the things we saw before, plus one more . . . . . First examine the precipice once again . . . What does it look like today? . . . . . Is the sun shining on it, or is rain falling on it? . . . . . And the craggy rocks below . . . are they in sunshine or shadow? . . . . . Do you notice anything on these craggy rocks today? . . . . . Any sea animals . . or plants . . anything at all . . . . . What about down around the bottom of the crags, are there starfish, or mussels? . . . . . Are there waves where these rocks meet the sea?

Now look out onto the ocean for the sloop . . . . . What is the water like today? . . . Notice the water's colors and texture . . . . . You can see the the sloop is near the obstacles. Watch as the sloop avoids them . . . .

Now the water and the air get a little rougher . . . . . The wind is coming up, and the waves are getting higher . . . . . You look out to the sloop and notice that it is careening . . . . . Watch as it careens . . . . . back and forth . . . . . The wind gets even stronger and rain begins to fall on the water and on the shore, and the sloop careens through the water . . . . Then the sun comes out, the wind dies down . . . . . and everything is just as it was when you first saw it today.

GROUNDING
In just a minute, when you open your eyes, I want you to represent the sloop careening through the water. Whatever you put down will be all right. I don't expect you to know the meaning of the word 'careen' yet; I want to see what you are doing with your own imagination. Include anything else that you wish in your drawing, and remember to draw only on page nine. Begin.

SHARING
Again, ask a student to look up the definition in the dictionary; then all draw or write the correct meaning of the word on page ten.

EVALUATION
Ask the students to look through their books, remembering the correct meaning for each of the words. If any are not sure of the words, this is their chance to review.

Now ask students to turn to the last blank page, page eleven. On this page, they are to write a single sentence, correctly using all five of this week's vocabulary words.

I grade this on a point system, giving one point for each word correctly and meaningfully used, and one more point for the overall sense of the sentence. Six points means an 'A,' five a 'B,' and so on.

SUGGESTIONS FOR OTHER VOCABULARY BOOKS
The lists provided here are intended to help you get started on other vocabulary books. For each one, you will need to write the script, using the sample Journey as a blueprint. Select lists of words from your study units. They will be more meaningful and have more carryover in your class.

Group the words according to a common topic so that the visualization and the sentence on Day Five will be coherent. The lists are purposefully too long, as you need only five words for each vocabulary book. Choose the five that you think would be best for use with your students, selecting those that you think most of the students will not know. Do not try more than five words per week in this manner.

♣ **Vocabulary Books**

RELATED VOCABULARY WORDS:

BUILDING
architect, parapet, girder, inaccessible, grandiose, design, cantilever, skyscraper, condominium, facade, blueprint, balcony, columns.

CAVES
stalactite, stalagmite, spelunker, devoid of light, fissure, chasm, grotto, cavern, soluble rock, expedition, labyrinth.

CIRCUS
barker, carousel, highwire act, sideshows, exhibition, ringmaster, ferocious, outlandish, venomous, exotic, roustabouts, prestidigitator.

DESERTS
erosion, mesa, desiccation, drought, arroyo, flash flood, barren land, tenacious plant life, sidewinder, prospector, cantankerous.

HIKING
knapsack, pitons, wilderness, rivulets, topographic map, foray, grueling climb, hazardous, provisions, ascend, monumental, buttes.

JUNGLE
menagerie, safari, expedition, explorer, profusion, flora and fauna, intrepid, ornithologist, amphibian, carnivore, herbivore.

OLD SHIPS
cargo, voyage, sheepshank, poop deck, bow, stern, starboard, keel, astrolabe, sextant, figurehead.

SPACE
horizon, trajectory, orbit, eclipse, contraption, experimental, spacecraft, communication, device, calculation, atmosphere, acceleration.

TRAINS
trestle, railroad ties, caboose, conductor, schedule, hoboes, highballing, freight, transport, express diner, hopper, tank car.

SECTION II

LITERATURE

12
Comprehension

RATIONALE
Teaching students to visualize as they read offers a most effective approach to teaching comprehension skills. Another is the use of higher levels of questions.

There are different kinds of questions to ask students, different not just in content, but in the kinds of thinking skills that the questions engender. Hilda Taba's Levels of Questioning presents a structure for many different categories of questions. As you expose your students to a greater variety of questions, their comprehension should deepen dramatically.

Taba identifies three basic kinds, or levels, of questions:
LEVEL 1, RECALL which encompasses questions concerning sheer rote, such as listing, matching, reciting, identifying.
LEVEL 2, PROCESSING which pertains to what students do with the information, including classifying, analyzing or synthesizing, explaining, comparing and contrasting.
LEVEL 3, APPLICATION which consists of creating something new from the material, such as model building, hypothesizing, predicting, and making generalizations.

At the first level, RECALL, nearly all of the questions have right answers. In the higher levels of PROCESS and APPLICATION, there can be many correct answers, and there can be legitimate differences of opinion among your students. It is these higher

DESCRIPTION
Students will read a common material. The teacher will lead a whole-class or small-group discussion, using Hilda Taba Levels of Questions.

PURPOSE
To improve reading comprehension through practice in high level thinking skills and to use literature in the practice.

SCHEDULING
Time needed for each lesson: 30-45 minutes
Number of lessons: One model for teacher-designed lessons. Schedule two in first week, then one per week for remaining weeks.

145

♣ Comprehension

MATERIALS NEEDED
For Each Student
A short selection of literature or non-fiction. It is also possible to do this activity from a selection that you have read aloud.

For The Teacher
Higher level questions to increase comprehension.

levels of questions that prod your students to gain a deeper comprehension of what they read.

When answering Level 2 and Level 3 questions, however, either orally or in written form, the students must use their own words and their own thinking skills in order to perform the task.

PREPARATION
- Select a story or non-fiction article that lends itself to thought-provoking discussion. Stories with a moral, myths, scientifically controversial subjects, and newspaper articles are all appropriate.

- Create questions. The heart of this activity starts with the teacher thinking of and writing out the questions for the selection that the students will be given. Do not expect to be able to invent such multi-level questions on the spur of the moment. It is rare to be able to spontaneously create thoughtful Level 2 and Level 3 questions. The questions need to be carefully prepared. Time spent on this part of the activity will produce the greatest benefit. And remember, if you conduct an insightful and mind-stretching oral discussion, then there will not be papers to correct; that time can be put to use in planning thought-provoking lessons.

Guidelines for creating these questions are provided below. I have listed all of the steps of Hilda Taba's Levels of Questioning. Next to each term that describes a thinking skill, I have included a sample question from a story that we all know and love.

Use Dr. Taba's list and the sample questions to help you create questions that will stimulate thinking and broaden comprehension.

Comprehension ✤

Taba's Levels	Sample Questions
Level 1: Recall	
COMPLETING:	Jack traded his mother's cow for _____.
COUNTING:	How may times did Jack climb the beanstalk?
DEFINING:	What is a beanstalk?
DESCRIBING:	Describe the special qualities of the giant's harp.
IDENTIFYING:	Which of the giant's treasures woke the giant?
LISTING:	List all of the things that Jack stole from the giant.
MATCHING:	I am going to say five things that were said in this story. Write down which Jack said, which his mother said, and which the giant said.
NAMING:	Name three things that Jack saw on his way to town.
OBSERVING:	What happened to the giant when Jack cut the beanstalk?
RECITING:	Repeat exactly what the giant said when he smelled Jack.
SELECTING:	Which of the following did Jack not steal: a harp, a goose, some beans, a pile of gold?
Level 2: Processing	
ANALYZING:	What clues tell that the giant was probably rich?
CLASSIFYING:	Which of the living characters in the story were not human?
COMPARING:	What are some ways that Jack's mother and the giant's wife were alike?
CONTRASTING:	What are some ways they were different?
DISTINGUISHING:	What was the point at which this story changed from one that could be true to one that had to be fiction?
EXPERIMENTING:	If the fellow who bought the cow had been all out of magic beans, what other magic could he have offered Jack? Keep in mind that whatever he gives Jack must eventually take him up into giant land, and also return him to earth.
EXPLAINING:	What made it possible for Jack to get up into the giant's world?

✣ Comprehension

GROUPING:	Name three characters from the story that belong together in some way, and tell how they belong together.
INFERRING:	If the giant had reached the earth safely, what do you think he would have done?
MAKING ANALOGIES:	Of the things you have in your garage or home, what is Jack's beanstalk most like?
ORGANIZING:	Here is a list of ten things that happened during the story. In one column list the events that happened *before* Jack climbed the beanstalk. In a second column list the events that happened *after* Jack climbed the beanstalk.

Level 3: Application

APPLYING A PRINCIPLE:	Jack discovered a good way to stop the giant from catching him. Using that same principle, what could he do if the giant were trying to chase him over a long wooden bridge?
EVALUATING:	Do you think that Jack's method of killing the giant was the best way to handle the problem? Why?
EXTRAPOLATING:	If Jack had a chance to visit the giant's castle one moretime before he was caught, what do you think he would have found that time?
FORECASTING:	What do you think Jack will do the next time his mother asks him to go to town to trade a cow?
GENERALIZING:	Jack's mother sent him to bed without any supper for trading the cow for a handful of beans. What do you think most mothers would have done?
HYPOTHESIZING:	Why do you think a giant would want to kill a boy like Jack before he had done anything wrong?
IMAGINING:	Imagine hiding inside of the giant's oven. What does it looks like in there?
JUDGING:	Do you think it was right for Jack to steal the giant's treasures?

While I have included all of Dr. Taba's categories and subcategories, I do not suggest that you need to try to think of questions from every category every time you use this activity. Remember that the point of the Taba list is merely to help you to be aware that there are many kinds of questions, and that students will learn to think and comprehend at a higher level if given frequent opportunities to do so.

- Distribute materials.
- Tell your students that in the discussion that follows you will not be looking for facts so much as opinions. Tell them that disagreement is more than acceptable; it is desirable.

CONDUCTING THE QUESTIONING SESSION

- Once you have prepared your questions on all levels, have your students read the selection. They can do this silently, or orally, or you can read the story to them. Reading aloud is especially appropriate if you want to expose them to selections of literature or non-fiction that are beyond the class's average reading level.
- Begin by asking questions only from Level 1. This is done so that all students will have a basic sense of the action of the story before you begin questions which ask them to build upon that foundation. Then, move on to Levels 2 and 3. All students need to have practice thinking at all three levels. In fact, your low achievers often show more skill at answering questions at Levels 2 and 3 than they do in Level 1. Give all students the opportunity to learn to think at higher levels.

While it is possible to ask students these questions in writing, I much prefer the oral mode. The class discussion approach stimulates more thought in students. As they hear each other's answers and then agree or disagree, students become more involved.

- If you find students are not paying attention to the discussion, you can use the paper/pencil method from "What Turtle," in which you ask the class a question, all respond on paper, and then discuss the responses. Follow this procedure with all your questions.

- Be sure to ask each question before you call on a given student. In this way, the entire class will be thinking.

❖ **Comprehension**

- Ask three or four more students whether they agree with the first answer or if they have a different idea. The thinking doesn't stop as soon as you call on one student. This technique is particularly effective when dealing with questions from Levels 2 and 3, as students seldom have the same answer to the questions from these levels.

EVALUATION

For major evaluation, assess during discussions and in written work in which students need more guidance and instruction in thinking at higher levels. You can then give them practice in these kinds of tasks using very easy, but interesting, reading material.

For formal grading, choose the check, plus, minus system based on effort.

13
Reading and Sharing Books

RATIONALE

If we want students to get hooked on reading, we must provide time for them to read in class. If we provide time for them to read only what we have selected, as is usually the case when a basal series is followed, then most of the students will not develop a strong interest in reading. Students need the opportunity to pursue books and stories that are of interest to them. A daily block of time for reading material of their own choosing is important so students can experience the pleasure of reading something that interests them personally. They see that you value reading when you give it a place of honor in the curriculum and when you take time to read yourself. Students learn valuable lessons about self-direction and self-motivation as they select their own books and their own reading goals.

The sharing process outlined in this chapter is chosen for its maximum benefit to students and its minimum burden of record-keeping for the teacher. In an efficient and enjoyable manner, this plan holds the students accountable for their use of silent reading time. They report to their peers and their teacher weekly and are usually eager to "take their turns." As students select their own materials, they develop their own tastes, interests, and enthusiasm for reading. No longer is the opportunity to read restricted to students who finish their work early.

DESCRIPTION
Students read independently self-selected books, twenty to thirty minutes daily. In the last ten minutes of the period, students share what they have been reading, while the class and the teacher ask a few questions.

PURPOSE
To expose students to a large variety of books by sharing them with their peers and to generate excitement and enthusiasm for reading.

SCHEDULING
Time needed for each lesson: 30-45 minutes
Number of lessons: Daily for the rest of the year.

♣ Reading and Sharing Books

MATERIALS NEEDED
For Each Student
A variety of books in a wide range of difficulty. If possible, create a room library.

For The Teacher
A Record Folder, which has an Individual Record Sheet for each student; a Reading Folder for each student, Reading Folder Sheets, and a Daily Book Sharing Schedule (see page 155).

PREPARATION
- Help each student select a book. Your librarian can help with this, and as you gain experience in literature, your ability to assist will quickly grow. As a classroom library is a big help, begin to create one if you possibly can. Possible sources of books include: central district or county school libraries which will sometimes loan fifty or a hundred books for several months at a time. I make these the backbone of the classroom library. Students can be asked to donate books they have bought and already read; they can inscribe the books as "donated to our school from . . ." Fund raising can be done by the class for book purchases. Grants may be available. Parent clubs can be asked for help. The school library may have additonal funds. Book clubs may offer a few free copies with class orders.
- Prepare the Record Folder, Reading Folders, and Daily Schedule as described below. Post the Daily Schedule in a prominent spot.
- Find a time in each school day in which students can read for a half-hour or more. Put a sign on the outside of your classroom door that says something like: DO NOT DISTURB: STUDENTS ARE READING.
- Explain to students about the rules during silent reading time. If students finish or wish to change books, they go quietly to your library and do so. Everyone reads, including you if possible.
- Set out the guidelines for the sharing time. Students will tell name and author of books and a few things that they liked about their books. Then the class and the teacher will ask a few questions. Sharing time should be brief, with five students sharing in about ten minutes.
- Set a specific time that students will be able to count on for silent reading of material that they have chosen. This can be twenty minutes a day, a half-hour a day, or forty-five minutes three times a week, but it should be clearly and specifically set up by you and uninterrupted by any other activities. Everyone reads during this time.

BOOK SHARING TIME
Each day one-fifth of the students report orally about what they have been reading. By week's end, every student has had one opportunity to report. Students are free to report anything they wish about their books, often telling of the plot, and sometimes reading favorite parts and sharing illustrations. The sharing should take only a minute or two, and when students are finished the teacher and the rest of the class can ask questions of the reporting student.

You may also wish to set a weekly focus for these brief reports: one week, students tell about their favorite character; another week, they read their favorite bit of dialogue or description; another week, they try to 'sell' the book to their peers.

BENEFITS TO BOOK SHARING TIME
- Because you know exactly what each student is reading at home and at school, you can make helpful suggestions for their next choices.
- Students convince each other to try books. When they hear a classmate's enthusiastic description of a book, they are much more likely to reach for it than for mandatory reading materials.
- Because students are not required to write a formal book report, they tend to read more and more.
- Questions from their peers about their books serve as a Grounding Activity.

RECORD KEEPING
I keep three kinds of records of the Silent Reading and Book Sharing:
1. Daily Schedule: Post the Daily Book Sharing Schedule (see page 155) on the wall to remind you which students are scheduled to share on each day of the week, and which actually did share on that day.

Reading and Sharing Books

Divide your class into five equal parts. The first fifth will report on Monday, the second fifth on Tuesday, the third fifth on Wednesday, and so on. When students report, put a check by their names. Thus, absent students can be picked up later in the week, or students whose turns fall on school holidays or assembly days can be assigned another day.

2. Record Sheets: Keep a Record Sheet Folder, (see page 157) which contains an Individual Record Sheet for each student. During book sharing, write the name of the book the student shares and any other information that might behelpful in evaluation. (Duplicate copies of the Individual Record Sheet for each student.)
3. Reading Folders: In a file easily accessible to students, keep a Reading Folder for each student with copies of the Reading Folder Sheet. When students finish books, they fill in information about those books. This record enables you to keep track of quality and quantity of books each student reads during the school year.

EVALUATION

The Individual Record Sheets enable you to constantly assess students' progress in their reading. As you review these sheets, you are able to determine if students are moving very slowly, or always choosing the same kind of book, or if they seem to need guidance or direction of any kind. The Reading Folders also help the students in another important kind of evaluation, self-evaluation. As they record their books in their folders, they develop a sense of pride in the number of books they have successfully and enjoyably completed.

For one student to have read four books in a quarter may be a much more significant event than for another to have read twenty or thirty. If you must, try to use grades to reward the great improvement you find in some low readers. Give the grade of 'A' only to students who have read a certain number of books and books from different categories, such as non-fiction, biography, fantasy, and historical fiction.

DAILY BOOK SHARING					
Student	Mon.	Tues.	Wed.	Thurs.	Fri.

READING FOLDER SHEET

Title _____
Author _____ Pages ___
Comment _____
_____
_____
_____

Title _____
Author _____ Pages ___
Comment _____
_____
_____
_____

Title _____
Author _____ Pages ___
Comment _____
_____
_____
_____

Title _____
Author _____ Pages ___
Comment _____
_____
_____
_____

Title _____
Author _____ Pages ___
Comment _____
_____
_____
_____

Title _____
Author _____ Pages ___
Comment _____
_____
_____
_____

Title _____
Author _____ Pages ___
Comment _____
_____
_____
_____

Title _____
Author _____ Pages ___
Comment _____
_____
_____
_____

INDIVIDUAL RECORD SHEET

Student's Name _____

Date _____ Book Title _____
Teacher Comments _____
_____
_____
_____

Date _____ Book Title _____
Teacher Comments _____
_____
_____
_____

Date _____ Book Title _____
Teacher Comments _____
_____
_____
_____

Date _____ Book Title _____
Teacher Comments _____
_____
_____
_____

Date _____ Book Title _____
Teacher Comments _____
_____
_____
_____

14
Homework Program

DESCRIPTION
Students will read their own literature selections every evening. Grades will be based on the amount read and verified by a parent.

PURPOSE
To develop a habit of daily reading, thereby increasing reading skills and vocabularies through practice and exposure.

SCHEDULING
Time needed for each lesson: 30-60 minutes
Number of lessons: Four per week at home.

RATIONALE
It is generally agreed that homework given to students should not be work that they do not yet understand. Homework should consist of what students already know. Independent reading falls easily into that category.

A most effective way for students to increase their reading skills and their love of reading is to read for a significant time regularly. Unfortunately, there is not enough time in the school day to do enough reading to accomplish this goal.

Therefore, you must set up a system which ensures that your students continue to read after the school day is ended. Any reading at all is acceptable: newspapers, magazines, cookbooks, even cereal boxes.

It is highly likely that, by reading from one-half hour to one hour every school night over the course of a year, your students will:

1. Develop a habit of reading on a regular basis that will carry on through the years.
2. Infect others in their family with that habit.
3. Read a far greater amount of material than they could possibly complete during school.

4. Be forced to find ways to discover material that is interesting to them, as it is to their own best interest to be reading materials that they enjoy when they must do it so often.
5. Increase their comprehension and their vocabularies by reading extensively.
6. Enjoy reading more and more as they engage in it more and more.

PREPARATION

- Explain to your students' parents at the parents' meeting usually held early in the year the nature of the reading homework. Tell them that the assignment for four school nights will hold for the duration of the year. This effectively squelches the students' chances of telling their parents that they have no homework, when both parents and children know full well the truth of the matter.
- In this nightly reading assignment, parents should begin to notice the progress their children are making, and be aware that you, as their children's teacher, are widening and deepening the children's reading abilities. Students who had previously never completed a single book usually begin reading five to ten books in a single quarter. Parents become proud of the amount and the quality of their children's reading, and they support this program.
- Start this program as soon as you judge your students are reading independently with fair comprehension. You can usually begin this segment and the book reading and sharing segment (Chapter 13) at the same time, as they both require the same level of independence in reading ability.
- Be sure that students have selected appropriate books. They may read the same one that they are reading at silent reading time in class, if they wish.
- Set aside a page in your grade book to record missing record sheets.

MATERIALS NEEDED
For Each Student
A weekly Homework Record Sheet and a self-selected book.

For The Teacher
A self-inking rubber stamp (with a star or other appealing design).

♣ Homework Program

- Talk to your students about the reasons for this homework program, and explain the rules and the grading system:
  1. Each day students take home reading books and their Homework Record Sheets.
  2. Each evening they are to read at least a half-hour, or longer. Then, they record the title and author, length of time, and the number of pages they read. A parent or other authority figure signs the day's record, confirming that the work was done.
  3. Every day the students bring their books and record sheets back to school. They may wish to use the record sheet as a bookmark.
  4. During silent reading time in class, students put the record sheets on their desks. While they are reading, go to each sheet and stamp the day's entry and signature with your rubber stamp. If any sheets are missing that day, make a note of it in your grade book. If students are busy one evening and make up by doing twice as much reading the next night, or over the weekend, I give them credit when the time is made up.

     This daily checking of the record sheet is an essential part of the reading homework program. If students know you are checking them every day, the program works very well. If they turn in their record sheets only once a week, the program may not work as well. Students seem to need this daily feedback and reinforcement in order to follow through on their homework assignment.
  5. On Mondays, students turn in their record sheets and get new ones. They can figure their own grades and enter them on their sheet. While double check their calculations, I find that students are even more successful in this program when they are responsible for grading their progress. After you record their grades, return their sheets which they keep in their folders.

Homework Record Sheet

Monday

Title _____ Author _____

Title _____ Author _____

Date _____ Parent Signature _____

Time Spent Reading: [HOURS | MINS]

[ ] TEACHER'S CHECK

Tuesday

Title _____ Author _____

Title _____ Author _____

Date _____ Parent Signature _____

Time Spent Reading: [HOURS | MINS]

[ ] TEACHER'S CHECK

Wednesday

Title _____ Author _____

Title _____ Author _____

Date _____ Parent Signature _____

Time Spent Reading: [HOURS | MINS]

[ ] TEACHER'S CHECK

Thursday

Title _____ Author _____

Title _____ Author _____

Date _____ Parent Signature _____

Time Spent Reading: [HOURS | MINS]

[ ] TEACHER'S CHECK

Weekend

Title _____ Author _____

Title _____ Author _____

Title _____ Author _____

Title _____ Author _____

Date _____ Parent Signature _____

Time Spent Reading: [HOURS | MINS]

Total Time for the Week: [HOURS | MINS] = [ ] GRADE

[ ] TEACHER'S CHECK

❖ **Homework Program**

EVALUATION
For the first quarter in this system, follow a simple rule that considers only the amount of time spent reading. Assume that any time verified by parental signature is genuine. To allow for make-up work, average the week's times. Be sure to inform students of this evaluation system so they can record their own grades.

The standard for the first quarter is:
A = at least one hour each for four days.
B = at least forty-five minutes each for four days.
C = at least one half-hour each for four days.
D = at least fifteen minutes each for four days.
F = any less than fifteen minutes each for four days.

In the second quarter, make the additional requirement that A's will be awarded only to students who pick at least two books from categories that they have not read before in the year. Some of these categories are: non-fiction, biographies, award-winning books, stories of other lands, historical fiction, poetry, fantasy, science fiction, adventure, western.

The students and I agree at the start of the new quarter on the categories that will be covered, and write that agreement in their Reading Record Folders. Take this grading system as only one way to approach a homework reading program. You may want to adjust the standards to fit your own class and style.

15
Oral Reading

RATIONALE

There are many valid reasons for reading daily to your class. Among the benefits are:
- Increased vocabulary through meaningful, contextual exposure to new words.
- Appreciation of good literature.
- Opportunity to introduce students to new authors, writers that they might never pick independently.
- Further chances for students to practice visualization while they listen.
- A verification of the value of reading by the importance it is given in the school day.
- A wealth of common stories you can use with your class for discussion, writing exercises, and higher levels of questions.
- Pure enjoyment by class and teacher alike.

Support and validation for reading to students can be found in educational research. In various studies we can also find increases in improved visual decoding and motor encoding, and improved reading comprehension. These results are found in classrooms where students are regularly read to.

At the junior high and high school level, oral reading can help fulfill requirements set by the school or by the State Department of Education regarding books that all students must read at vari-

DESCRIPTION
Teacher will read daily to students for 15-20 minutes. Selections will be interesting, high quality, and a bit above the reading level of most of the class.

PURPOSE
To stimulate interest in books, increase vocabularies, provide models of correctly spoken language in a variety of styles, and motivate students to read more.

SCHEDULING
Time needed for each lesson: 15-20 minutes. Number of Lessons: One daily, selected by the teacher, preferably for most of the year.

163

Oral Reading

ous grade levels. Oral reading of classics can take the pain and frustration out of trying to force poorer readers through a book that gives them great difficulty and little pleasure. After all, it is not likely that students' hunger for reading and literature will be increased by forcing them through weeks of torturous struggle.

Instead, you can read at any pace you like with your whole class, adding visualization exercises, writing assignments, and vocabulary development lessons as you go. Your whole class then acquires a common background of some classic literature. Not all of your oral reading should be of this genre, however. At the beginning of the year especially, students need to be read lighter material so they can become accustomed to listening for longer periods of time. They need encouragement to visualize so that your words come to life as they listen.

MATERIALS NEEDED
For Each Student
Absolutely nothing.

For The Teacher
A good book.

SELECTING BOOKS

Develop sources for good books. Enlist your school or county librarians to watch for great books at your grade level. Although they will have lists of award-winning books, these are not always the best for reading aloud.

Your students are also a good resource for books. They will begin to bring books they have particularly enjoyed. Even though these are not always appropriate for reading aloud, you sometimes will get a wonderful book this way. If a student has gone to the trouble to recommend a book and it is not a good read-aloud, read a few pages to the class and then ask who would like to finish it for independent reading. This kind of book-selling can also be a planned part of the oral reading program.

There are many publications that publish annotated book lists. A few of these sources are:

Adventuring with Books. National Council of Teachers of English. (A book list for pre-K through 8th grade.)
For Reading Out Loud. Margaret Mary Kimmel, and Elizabeth Segel. (A guide to sharing books with children.)
High Interest Easy Reading. Marian White. (For junior and senior high.)
Literature and Story Writing. California State Department of Education.
Literature for Today's Young Adults. Kenneth Donelson and Aleen Pace Milsen.
The Read Aloud Handbook. Jim Trelease. (How and when to read aloud, and a summary of a number of books.)

After you have selected your book, by all means read it first yourself. If you do not, you may run into many embarrassing moments in front of your class. Some important criteria are:

1. Do you like it? You will be reading this book for many weeks, and if it is not fun for you, it will not be fun for your students.
2. Is the vocabulary appropriate for your students? There is merit in a vocabulary that is somewhat more difficult than the level they are accustomed to hearing, but if every paragraph has two or three key words that students do not know, they will lose interest.
3. Is the topic appropriate for your students and for reading aloud? Sometimes midway through a book you may suddenly come upon an attempted molestation, or some other kind of scene that you may not be comfortable reading aloud. Be prepared. Know what is coming. If the book has enough value to go ahead regardless, you can paraphrase or summarize.
4. Is the style one that can be read aloud easily? Some literature is so full of complex sentences that it is all but impossible to read aloud smoothly. Some has so much dialogue, with no indication of who is talking, that everyone, including the reader, is soon perplexed. Books with many dialects should be carefully considered.
5. Can you handle the style of the humor or the emotional content? If the style of humor in the book is not the kind that you find amusing, or if

you think that you cannot read the straight parts with a straight face because you know what is coming next, then this book is not for you.

If your dog just died, you might not want to read a story like *Old Yeller*. You may not be able to get through the sad parts without openly weeping. There is nothing wrong with having some tears when a story is genuinely sad. In fact it is good for your students to see your compassion. But your grief should not interfere with their concentration on the story.

Also, consider your prejudices. If you have some that you do not wish to pass along, you might want to avoid books that deal with related issues. Remember, if you the book you pick just doesn't work once you start reading it, ask if someone in your class would like to finish it, and go on to your next selection. If no one wants it, you know you were wise to drop it!

YOUR BEHAVIOR

If you are confident in reading aloud and you know that your students respond, then go right ahead and start reading. If not, there are books you can find that give suggestions for improving your read-aloud skills. Or you can seek out classes in oral reading, drama, or story-telling. The classes will be fun for you, and your students will reap the benefits as well.

One of the most effective aids is practice. Read to your own children, your husband, wife or housemate, or in front of the mirror. Read into a tape recorder and see how you sound. Then adjust and try it again.

Sometimes you will need to practice even if you are skilled at reading aloud. To do justice to dialogue, especially if there are accents involved, you will be wise to practice.

When you are finally standing in front of your class, and out of your mouth comes a believable southern drawl or a passable French accent, the looks on your students' faces are well worth all of the effort you take in preparation.

STUDENT BEHAVIOR

I strongly recommend allowing no activity other than listening to you. The object in reading aloud is that students recreate the action and settings of the story in their own minds, bringing the book to life. Give your class the greatest possible chance to do this by allowing no barriers between them and the words from you. Some teachers prefer not to even show a book's illustrations until they have entirely finished reading the book.

TIME FRAME

I hope that you begin reading aloud on the first day of school and stop on the last. While there are occasions in your daily schedule when something must be sacrificed for the sake of time, please do not let this activity always be the first to go. Sometimes we begin to think of oral reading as a time filler. Students tend not to consider it a part of their real instructional program. Once you become convinced of the true value of this opportunity to share and participate in good literature, your actions will reflect your belief, and your students will begin to see this activity in a new light.

The number of minutes you spend each day will vary with the grade level and the interest level of the material you are reading. I recommend at least twenty minutes a day. If you decide to read aloud past the time that you have set up with your class, you can be sure that students will be on their best behavior, hoping that nothing will distract you or cause you to stop.

It is always effective to quit for the day at the most interesting moment, leaving the students hanging on the edges of their seats. Be prepared for moans and groans. There are other times when it is wise to stop in the middle of a boring section, especially if you sense that you are losing their interest. Perhaps you can read ahead that evening and summarize the next day. You do not have to read every word of every book; sometimes authors offer long descriptive passages which are interesting when read silently, but confusing or tedious when read aloud.

❖ Oral Reading

ALTERNATIVES TO READING ALOUD

Perhaps you have tried every possible assistance that you can think of to help you read aloud effectively, and you still cannot hold your students' interest. Or perhaps you would like a break, or some variety in between books. Here are some alternatives to reading aloud:

- Trade with another teacher. Find a teacher who is an effective oral reader, and chances are excellent that he or she will be eager to trade classes for twenty minutes a day, while you share some of your unique and special talents with the other class.

- Tell stories. The art of storytelling extends far beyond that of written literature. Storytelling has been with us since the beginning of mankind. It is an art and a delight, and well worth sharpening your skills and learning good stories. Myths and fairy tales lend themselves particularly well to this delivery style.

  Storytelling can also be a way to share the plots of books and plays that are beyond the reading comprehension level of your class. The stories of Shakespeare can be told at grade levels far lower than those that can read his works.

  Don't neglect the funny story. And if you have some really exciting true stories of your adventures, this is an appropriate time for them.

- Play recorded instrumental music of high quality. Students can shut their eyes and see whatever appears in their imaginations, and then ground by writing or drawing when the music is over. Or, you might encourage students to draw while they listen.

- Radio plays. Many radio stations broadcast old radio plays on a regular basis. The Lone Ranger, the Shadow, and the Green Hornet are among the old favorites once again on the airways. If you have the equipment for taping at home, bring a broadcast into your class.

Students can visualize during the play, and then complete some kind of grounding assignment that they have been prepared for before the broadcast began. You might ask them to draw the setting or the characters, or to write a detailed description. Or turn the story into comic book form. Be sure to check on the current law covering such taping.

- Prerecorded literature. There are many recordings of excellent actors and actresses reading good literature. Listen to these yourself before you share them with your class, as some styles may seem stilted to your students. Turn down the lights or to use blindfolds during this activity.

  This activity can be done just for its own sake, or with the addition of grounding activities. If possible, make available the actual piece of literature that is being read so that students can make the association.

- Picture books. Just because you are working with upper grades, or even high school students, do not overlook picture books, the ones that are kept in the section of the library designated for young children. Many of these books are absolutely astonishing. Your librarian can direct you to the books that are of excellent quality in both writing and illustration and of genuine interest and value to older children. Students of all ages enjoy these.

  There is an added bonus in the picture books with no words at all. These wordless picture books are a high-interest invitation to your students to write a caption to each picture to tell their interpretation of the story.

  At first your older students may resist reading "baby books," but if you introduce these books by reading them at oral reading time, they will soon be circulating around the room at silent reading time as well.

- "Selling" books. Occasionally, do not read a whole book. From time to time, just read a chapter or two, enough to capture the students' interest. Then ask who would like to finish during silent reading time. This is a great way to get some new books circulating in your class.

❖ Oral Reading

- Capitalize on a book. After your whole class has listened to a good book, you may sometimes choose to use the book as the basis for work in comprehension skills and in writing skills.

  For example, students can analyze plot and character, sequence the important events of the story, examine the elements of a good plot, or write opinions about what was expressed by the author. Plays and skits can center around scenes from the book.

CONCLUSION

It is in reading that the essential ideas of human civilization are passed from generation to generation. And it is through reading that bright new ideas are engendered. This manual will give you a foundation for bringing meaning and depth to the teaching of reading.

The visualization segment is meant to give students the ability to truly see and fully comprehend what they read. The literature component will then provide you with a strong framework of classroom management so that you can allow exploration of literature on an expansive and individual basis.

When the teaching of reading emphasizes joy and excitement, you give your students a priceless gift. The love of reading enriches their lives and, in turn, will enrich our nation and our world.

BIBLIOGRAPHY

Anderson and Hidde. "Imagery and Sentence Learning." *Journal of Educational Psychology* 62 No. 6 (1971): 526.

Arbuthnot, May Hill, ed. *Time for Fairy Tales, Old and New.* New York: Scott and Foresman and Co., 1961.

Applebee, Arthur N., Judith A. Langer, and Ina V.S. Mullis. *Who Reads Best?* Princeton: Educational Testing Service (1988): 5-6.

Bussis, Anne and Edward Chittendon. "Research Currents: What the Reading Tests Neglect." *Language Arts* 64, 3, (March 1987): 303.

Campbell, Joseph. *Hero with a Thousand Faces.* New York: Princeton University Press, 1949.

Durkin, Dolores. "What Classroom Observations Reveal About Reading Comprehension Instruction." In *Reading Research Revisited*, edited by L.M.Gentile, M.L. Kamil, and J.S. Blanchard. Columbus, Ohio: Charles Merrill, 1983.

Escondido Union School District Board of Education. *Mind's Eye,* Prepared by Marjorie Pressley, Margaret Horton, James Retson, Wilhelmine Nielson. Escondido, California, 1979.

Houston, Jean and Robert Masters. *Mind Games.* New York: Viking Press, 1975.

Hunter, Madeline. Lecture on Right/Left Brain. State Department of Education Conference. Sacramento, California 1979.

_____ *Motivation Theory for Teachers.* El Segundo, California: TIP Publications, 1967.

_____ *Reinforcement Theory for Teachers.* El Segundo, California: TIP Publications, 1967.

_____ *Teach for Transfer.* El Segundo, California: TIP Publications, 1971.

_____ *Teach More—Faster!* El Segundo, California: TIP Publications, 1969.

Leonard, George. *Education and Ecstasy.* New York: Delacorte Press, 1968.

Maker, C. June. *Teaching Models in Education of the Gifted.* Rockville, Maryland: Aspen Publishing Inc., 1982.

McCormick, Sandra. "Should You Read Aloud to Your Child?" *Language Arts* 54, No. 2 (1977).

McKenna, Alexis. *Doodling Your Way to Better Recall, or Mapping Your Way to Memory.* Tucson, Arizona: Zephyr Press, 1982.

Office of the Los Angeles County Superintendent of Schools. 1978. Equal Opportunity in the Classroom. Prepared by Sam Kerman, Tom Kimball, Vera Tolmasov, Denise Yates. Los Angeles.

Ornstein, Robert. *The Nature of Human Consciousness: A Book of Readings.* San Francisco: W.H. Freeman, 1973.

Pikulski, John. "Curriculum Update." Interview with author. Association for Supervision and Curriculum Development. Alexandria, Virginia, September 1987.

Reading: A Conversation with Kenneth Goodman. New York: Scott, Foresman & Co., 1976.

Samples, Robert. *The Metaphoric Mind.* Reading, Massachusetts: Addison-Wesley, 1976.

_____ *Open Mind/Whole Mind.* Rolling Hills Estates, California: Jalmar Press, 1987.

Sylwester, Robert. Lecture on Brain Hemisphericity. Presented at Redding Reading Conference. Redding, California, 1982.

Bibliography

Taba, Hilda. *The Dynamics of Education: A Methodology of Progressive Educational Thought.* London: Kegan Paul, Trench, Trubner and Co., 1932.

Tom, Chow Loy. "What Teachers Read to Pupils in the Middle Grades." Ph.D. Dissertation, Ohio State University, 1969.

Vitale, Barbara Meister. *Free Flight: Celebrating Your Right Brain.* Rolling Hills Estates, California: Jalmar Press, 1986.

_____ *Unicorns are Real: A Right-Brained Approach to Learning.* Rolling Hills Estates, California: Jalmar Press, 1982.

Walter, W. Grey. *The Living Brain.* New York: Norton, 1953.

Webster's Third New International Dictionary, s.v. "archetype."

Williams, Linda Velez. *Teaching for the Two-Sided Mind: A Guide to Right Brain/Left Brain Education.* New York: Simon and Schuster, Inc., 1986.

ADDITIONAL RESOURCES FROM ZEPHYR PRESS TO ENRICH YOUR PROGRAMS—

MAGIC TRUMPETS: The Story of Jazz for Young People
by Stephen Longstreet (1989)
This exhilarating and informative story of jazz will bring color and breadth to the study of American history. More than 75 bold illustrations combined with captivating text make this book enjoyable reading even for hard-to-interest students. Ideal for libraries, classrooms, and as a gift! Grades 7-Adult.
ZB12-W $16.95

The KNOW IT ALL Resource Book for Kids
by Patricia R. Peterson (1989)
Now your students can have all the answers with KNOW IT ALL— the greatest classroom resource since the dictionary! How do you change decimals to percents? How do you remember how many days are in each month? These and hundreds of frequently asked questions are answered in this book. Grades 2-Adult.
ZB14-W $12.95

A MATHEMATICAL MYSTERY TOUR: Higher-Thinking Math Tasks
by Mark Wahl (1988)
This unique approach to learning math presents hands-on tasks that pay attention to learning styles and utilize the right hemisphere of the brain. Find out how pineapples, pinecones, pyramids, prime numbers, and planets all march to the same amazing numbers. Grades 5-12.
ZB06-W $19.95

MYSTERY TOUR GUIDE NEWSPAPER
This follow-along newspaper accompanies the book. One copy is needed for each participant.
ZB07-W . . . . $6.95 (set of 5 newspapers)

KIDVID: Fun-damentals of Video Instruction
by Kaye Black (1989)
Even "camera shy" teachers can bring video instruction into the classroom. Here's an easy-to-use guide for video production with nine fully prepared lessons—from the basics to hands-on experience with video equipment. Grades 4-8.
ZB13-W $13.95

SMART ART: Learning to Classify and Critique Art
by Patricia Hollingsworth, Ed.D., and Stephen F. Hollingsworth (1989)
This program takes readers on an imaginary visit through an art museum to teach students how to—
◆ Classify and critique art
◆ Use a variety of thinking skills
◆ Acquire art vocabulary
◆ Develop aesthetic understanding
Features 35 black-and-white and four full-color art reproductions. Grades 3-8.
ZB09-W $12.95

WORD FOR WORD: Creative Thinking Projects for Building Vocabulary
by Sue Clements Hovis and Bonnie Domin (1988)
Ten units in one book! You'll have more than 200 student-centered activities to build vocabulary in these areas— money, art, sports, weather, and more. You can incorporate any of these units into math, science, or social studies curricula, or use them on their own for a language arts unit. Grades 5-8.
ZB10-W $12.95

To order, write or call—

ZEPHYR PRESS
3865 East 34th Street, #101
P.O. Box 13448-W
Tucson, Arizona 85732-3448
(602) 745-9199

You can also request a free copy of our current catalog showing other learning materials that foster whole-brain learning, creative thinking, and self-awareness.